HIRED HAND

JOHN HANSEN

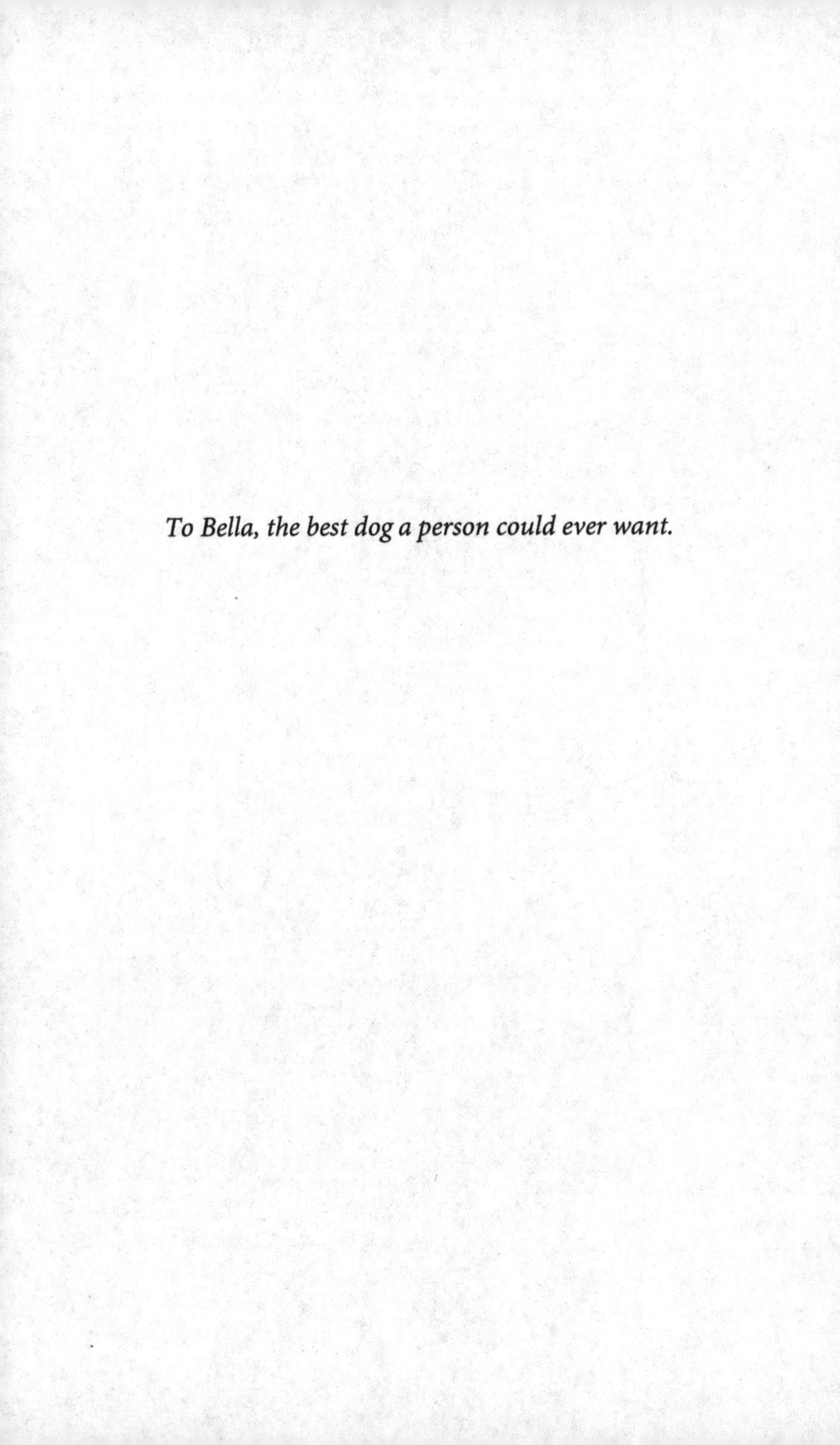

To Bella, the best dog a person could ever want.

PREFACE

I grew up on a ranch in southern Idaho in the 1950s and 60s. During that time, I worked on not only our place but other farms and ranches as well. In those days there seemed to be a class of men content to spend their lives as hired hands. Some of these men were married and good family men. Others, on the other hand, had very little to show for their efforts. They'd work for a couple of months and "go to town" and drink their wages. For some of these men it was a sad existence. What is equally as sad, in my opinion, is that these working men once so critical to agriculture just don't seem to exist anymore. It's a social phenomenon that I've frequently thought about. Just this past summer this issue was highlighted when a friend of ours told us that they could not find anyone to buck bales for $15 an hour. I was dumbfounded as back in the day I got a penny a bale. Hence, my motivation to write "HIRED HAND."

HIRED HAND

It was a little past midnight and darker than the inside of a closed lid coffin. The lights were coming fast, real fast. Too damned fast for pothole ridden County Road 32. Deputy Hank Childers who had been listening to country music while fighting to stay awake reached for his radar gun. He sighed: "Damn people. Don't they read the paper." Just last week a California tourist ran into one of Bill Rogers' Hereford bulls in broad daylight. Killed the bull and launched the tourist's wife through the windshield. The ambulance stopped just long enough in Pinetop for the one and only doctor there to shake his head as if the woman was as good as dead. "Better get on down to Bozeman. Maybe they can do something for her." That had been six days ago, and the woman was still in the hospital. Her husband, his newly acquired hotshot lawyer from Billings, Bill Rogers and the county's District Attorney had come close to fisticuffs over the validity of Montana's open range law. Childers grimaced as he read the numbers on the radar gun. "Are you shitin' me? Ah hundert and two on this goat trail." His heart was pounding as he fired up his '64 Dodge pickup, flipped on the headlights, and the red light on top, for whatever good that might do. It was about three hundred yards down the gravel road where his pickup had been parked to where it entered CR32. Childers shook his head and braked just short of the intersection. "Ain't no way this asshole is gonna stop for my red gumball."

And, in the next instant, the car flashed like a long-forgotten memory through Childers' headlights. It was loud, scary loud. The car parted the night air with such force that tiny bits of crumbly asphalt flipped onto the deputy's windshield with one piece coming in his open window striking him on the cheek. For a moment he sat there considering the futility of catching the speeder. In the distance he could still hear the car's straight pipes and see its taillights. In the off chance that he could reach the dispatch he keyed his mike. But it was dead quiet save for the crickets in the sage and grass outside and his heart thumping his eardrums. He sighed again, deep and angry. The wheels of his pickup shot gravel until they violently screeched upon contacting the pavement of CR32. He flipped on his siren and stabbed the gas pedal running the truck through its gears. It was a moonless night. He was over-driving his headlights, which he knew was foolish. He glanced down at the speedometer. "Ninety-five. This is bullshit. Damned county. You'd think in this day and age they'd have enough repeaters so I could call for some help." He drove on screaming through the blackness imagining another one of Rogers' escaped cows standing in the road. It played out in his mind as clear as if it was a movie on the big screen at the Chief Theater in Placerville. He'd hit the cow a glancing blow trying to avoid it, lose control of his pickup and roll three times getting thrown out and killed in the process. It'd be front page news just like the California tourists had been in the weekly Placerville Gazette. Hank's common sense shouted out to him. *Ought to just shut 'er down and go on about my business. No one will be the wiser. Besides, anybody wanting to get away this bad might not be a person to tangle with in the middle of the night by yourself.* He felt his right foot ease up on the gas and the pickup begin to slow. It was like a smarter version of him had taken over. The less smarter side was glad but, in the same instant, he spontaneously grumbled, "Aw shit." The speeder's taillights had suddenly gotten bigger, bolder and brighter. "What the hell is he doing?" And then the red dots disappeared. To the right of where they'd just been a spear of white light erupted. Childers sighed. "The sonovabitch has turned off. Why would he do that? Ain't no pavement there. I'll catch his sorry ass." But the white light pierced the darkness like a shooting star. Childers looked down at the speedometer. It read 45. He frowned and cursed himself as he downshifted to third and mashed the accelerator to the floor. The engine was winding tighter and tighter, until at 82 miles per hour, Childers slammed the gearshift into fourth. He no sooner did this when a sign on his right went by too fast for him to read. He cursed aloud simultaneous to jamming on the truck's brakes while sliding past the Bear Creek Road turnoff. The transmission cried out as he tried too soon to grind it into reverse. "Oh C'mon, you sonovabitch." And then the pickup began to move backwards. Its headlights revealed blue smoke hanging above black skid marks on the pavement. The smell of burnt rubber floated in through the pickup's open window. Childers hated the smell. Always had, but it paled in comparison to the effects of the dust from the graveled Bear Creek Road. It was like fog rolling into the cab of his pickup. The dust was suffocating. In five cranks he had the window rolled up. Still, he could not see much further than about a hundred feet. His common sense told him that he should go slow, which he did for a time. And then a crossing wind out of the north betrayed the location of the speeder. It was a sudden stiff breeze that carried the floury dust out over the sagebrush and allowed it to settle where it liked. Up ahead, maybe a half mile, were the red dots. Childers laughed. "Alright mister, I've got you now." He again shifted into third gear and stepped down hard on the gas. The pickup momentarily fishtailed before he counter steered and shifted to fourth gear at about 65 miles per hour. An awareness, or feeling, had come over him that this was a contest between good and evil and good had just mustered its resources to clear the dust. Childers was determined to not squander this opportunity. He was gaining on the red dots, this person who had no respect for the law, when suddenly the wind died down and the dust returned. A mental picture, however, had fixed itself in Childers mind. The red dots were straight out from him. Straight as an arrow they were. He knew this for a fact as he had driven the Bear Creek Road in the daylight many times before. So, he pressed on. His siren was wailing and red light pulsating in the darkness. He was doing close to 70 miles per hour, the dust not quite as thick as it had been. And then he saw it, just barely in the dust and darkness. Unlike the speeder who never slowed at all, Childers tried to stop but he was well beyond the broken barricade and "Bridge out" sign before he could get his foot on the brakes.

The canal was about fifteen feet wide. There was apparently adequate incentive for the speeder to roll the dice. He hit the barricade while pushing his car for even more speed. Fifty yards later he sailed over the chasm landing on the other side with a loud crashing bang. The speeder's car stalled. It was damaged, to what extent he did not know. He was trying desperately to start it when, in his rear-view mirror, he saw the swirling red light atop the headlights coming fast. And, as if that had not put the fear of going to the county lockup in him, the ear-piercing siren of Childers' pickup was getting louder and louder. The speeder reached for his door handle. "That dumbass is gonna land right on my car." But then, before he was completely out of the car, the realization of what was going to happen hit him. Relief that he wouldn't be caught was short-lived as the deputy's pickup impaled itself in the far bank of the canal. "Holy shit. Sonovabitch. Why didn't he stop?" The speeder felt his bowels begin to loosen. Fear was on the verge of having its way with him when the dark unconscionable side of him shot back. "What a fool. Stupid shit." He banged the hood of his car with his fist and kicked at the gravel with his cowboy boots. And then his instinct to survive took hold, distancing itself from what little conscience he had. The deputy's siren did not survive the crash, but his red light did and now its mis-directed strobe was rotating upward into the night sky like a searchlight. The nearest ranch house was about a mile away. Most likely they'd be asleep and if his car hadn't popped the left front tire, he'd just drive off assuming his car would start. What he did next came to him like someone else was in charge of his body. He opened his car's trunk and took out the lug wrench and started for the red light. To break it meant he would have to jump down into the canal which fortunately for him, was dry.

Hank Childers was bad off, but not to the point he couldn't hear the speeder's boots crunching through the gravel coming his way. He was pinned in the cab. The steering column had crushed his chest and something sharp had penetrated his thigh. He could not see the wound, but he could feel the blood pulsating almost in tempo with the whirring of the red light. Suddenly, to his left he heard something hit the ground followed by cursing. It was only natural to call out. Childers moaned. "Help me, please."

There were crickets and the whirring rotations of the red light and silence.

Childers whimpered. "Please, help me. I don't want to die."

The speeder's voice was devoid of hope. "Nobody does."

Childers sobbed. His tone suggested he knew that it was pointless to beg for help from the speeder. He fumbled for the strap holding his pistol in its holster. Then there was plastic and glass shattering and it became dark and quiet. Not long after, Childers felt a panicky drowsiness come over him. He did not fight it.

CHAPTER TWO

At about the same time Hank Childers was bleeding out on Bear Creek Road, Teddy Walker was in the Sawtooth Club on Pinetop's Main Street intently peeling the label from his fifth bottle of Olympia beer. It was his habit to do this when he was in deep thought and there was no one else to talk to but the bartender and some strangers he did not know. They were debating, or maybe not so much a debate as it was voicing their opinions, on the *worthless damned hippies* that were protesting the Vietnam war. They were three stools down from Teddy at the end of the bar next to the window facing the street. He didn't mind that they hadn't invited him into their conversation as he'd been in the big war. The war that most everybody agreed was necessary unless we wanted to be speaking German or Japanese. He didn't really like to think about the war or how his life had been back then, but these guys were a notch or two louder than the Hank Williams tune coming from the jukebox beyond the pool table across the room. Teddy paused in his peeling and took a long drink of his beer. In that instant his mind went back to that day in 1942.

"But Ma, if you sign for me they'll let me in," begged Teddy.

Teddy's mother, Agnes Kinney, said nothing as she put the Lucky Strike in her right hand to her lips and drew on it deeply. She held the smoke in her lungs and stared at Teddy

8

in a thoughtful but irritated way. Finally, she exhaled. "Is living here that bad, Teddy?"

Even through the cloud of gray smoke that shrouded his mother's face, he could see that she was tired. Her green eyes were always bloodshot from lack of sleep, and maybe too much booze, and the crow's feet at their corners didn't help. He came back, "You know things would be better if I wasn't here."

For a moment, that was too long for anything she might say after it to be credible, Agnes looked at Teddy from where she sat in a brown padded chair with white stuffing protruding from each of its armrests. She said, her right elbow resting on the chair with her forearm cocked in the air to allow the smoldering cigarette smoke an avenue of escape: "Teddy, we've been over this. Tom cares about you."

"Oh bullshit, Ma. You know that ain't so."

"He does, Teddy. He does."

Teddy scoffed. "He don't even care about you."

Agnes remained quiet tearing up just short of full blown crying and looked out the window to the snow covered mountains. The fire in the wood stove next to the padded chair popped and crackled. She took another drag from her cigarette and blew the smoke away, allowing the silence between them to validate what Teddy had just said.

Teddy now felt like a worthless shit, but he did not go to her. They'd never been much for hugging, or *I love you's*. He stayed where he was, standing in the middle of their tiny living room in the dumpy old clapboard house that came with the $300.00 a month wages that his stepfather earned as Jess Whitworth's hired hand. Finally, he said, "I'm sorry, Ma."

Agnes continued to stare out the window for a time before saying, "It's cold outside."

Teddy was perplexed at his mother's response but said simply, "Yeah, it is."

With her eyes still locked on the snowy mountain to the east of the house, she came back, "Nice and warm in here don't ya think?"

"Yeah," he said as he looked out the window wondering if maybe he was missing something. The winter sun was about to call it quits for the day. Just the top of the mountain where the trees gave way to steep rock that God had splashed with purple and orange was in the light, all else was shadowy.

At last, she looked at him, "Got a beef roast in the oven. Got spuds and carrots and onions with it too. You can smell it, can't you Teddy?"

"Yes, Ma'am."

Agnes put the cigarette to her mouth, drawing on it like it gave her confidence, and when the smoke exited her lungs creating a roily cloud between them she said, "There are more important things in life than love."

Teddy's first impulse was to disagree. But then he recalled how it had been when it was just him and his mother living with Grandma until things blew up there and they moved to a dingy apartment above the Owl Café where Agnes waited tables. He recalled too, the times the café owner "slept over." They had plenty to eat and gas money until one day, not long after his mother went out with Tom Kinney and he slept over, it all ended, So, here they'd been for the past three years living in the hired hand's house on the Whitworth ranch. Teddy saw that his mother's eyes were still watery. He said, "It's too bad life has to be that way."

Agnes stubbed her cigarette out in the ashtray sitting on an end table next to the chair, sighed, and then got to her feet. "Yeah, it is, isn't it." And then she added, "The wood box needs fillin'."

CHAPTER THREE

It was a little past six o'clock and almost dark when the green '36 Chevy pickup that Tom Kinney drove pulled up outside. He parked next to a black '32 Ford pickup which was his own. Agnes' red '31 Plymouth coupe sat on the west side of the house just outside the hog wire and wood post fence that defined the yard. It needed a new transmission. *Damned near a month's wages to fix it*, Tom had told her. So, there it sat under the big cottonwood tree now for over a year. Weeds had grown up around it and it was peppered unmercifully with bird crap.

They could see one another, Teddy and Tom, through the picture window in the living room. Teddy knew, from past experience, that it would rankle Tom seeing him sitting there in his gray Elkhorn Pirates tee shirt and Levi's listening to the radio. It wouldn't matter that the wood box was full and he'd split more wood for tonight stacking it neatly in the wood shed. And he'd washed and dried some dishes that his mother had asked him to do. No, what mattered to Tom was there was six inches of snow on the ground and the temperature was 18 degrees and he was outside and Teddy was in the warmth of the house doing nothing.

Tom stepped through the opening in the fence where a gate should have been and took a couple of steps on the worn down path in the snow that led to the front door and then paused. He turned his head to the side and put his finger to first one nostril and then the other to clear his nose. He looked up as he ran the back of his hand across his black droopy moustache. It was at this point he caught Teddy looking at him. He frowned. Teddy looked away. *Oh shit, here we go.*

Jack Benny was announcing his next act on the radio when Teddy heard Tom stomping his feet on the rickety wooden landing just outside the door. And then the door opened allowing a surge of cold air and Tom inside. Teddy thought to say, *Hey Tom*, but he didn't, keeping his eyes on the radio instead. At the same time, he sensed Tom was staring hard at the wood box in the kitchen as he hung his gray Stetson and coat on wall pegs to his right.

Agnes appeared in the archway to the kitchen. She did not go to Tom and kiss him *hello* and *inquire how was your day*? She'd given up that pretense not long before her car broke down. Wiping her hands on her apron, she came no further. "Supper's ready when you are."

"Colder 'n ah witch's tit out there. Can't keep the ice chopped outta the upper field's water hole."

Agnes shook her head slightly. She'd heard the same complaint at noon, but she said, "It's gotta be tough as cold as it is."

"Your damned right it is. I slipped into the crik this afternoon. Went in up to my knees. Soaked my Levi's and long-johns. Went down my boots. Feet are still so damned cold I can hardly feel 'em."

It came to Teddy that he could score some points with Tom if he was to sympathize with him. Reluctantly, he looked away from the old radio with its ornately carved cathedral wood casing and caught Tom's eye. "Jess wouldn't let ya come home and change?"

Tom snorted. "Shit, boy, we had work to do. It's four miles up there bucking snow drifts two feet deep in places. And we still had to go get a load of hay and feed that bunch."

He paused and shook his head in disgust. "Not everybody can sit around in a nice warm house listening to the radio all day."

Before Teddy could say anything, Agnes stepped from the kitchen. "Supper's ready."

Teddy got up from the couch and started for the kitchen as Tom sat on the wooden chair by the door unbuckling his overshoes. Tom looked at him and frowned like he wasn't deserving of supper. Teddy pretended he hadn't seen what Tom had done and took a seat at the table.

Agnes sat down across from him. She had an almost fearful look on her face as she glanced toward the living room before coming back to Teddy. She leaned forward, her face devoid of any makeup and her brown shoulder length hair appeared dull and shiny owing to the fact they didn't bathe as often as they should due to the house being on a septic system. They'd all been there when Jess Whitworth had told them, with a laugh, *mind your flushes or you'll be diggin' a new cesspool.* Agnes whispered: "Don't antagonize him, Teddy. He's already on the prod."

Teddy bobbed his head and scoffed. "When isn't he?"

Agnes frowned but said nothing as the two of them sat there listening to Tom's mumbled cursing while he struggled to pull his boots off. And then there were steps towards the bathroom, splashing in the toilet and moments later a flush. And then the pulsing of the coffee pot on the wood stove behind Teddy caught Agnes' eye. She abruptly stood up, a panicked look on her face realizing that supper wasn't entirely ready as Tom's coffee had just started to perk. Her hand was poised next to the pot, monitoring the color of the pulses in the lid's glass bubble.

It was hard for Teddy not to watch Tom's approach, as he appeared fixated on Agnes' backside. She was slender and not especially buxom. Here on the ranch her winter attire was often what she had on today, men's Levi's and a blue flannel shirt. The jeans were snug, revealing, probably worthy of gossip in town. Nonetheless, Teddy didn't care for the way Tom was looking at his mother since they rarely kissed or held hands or said that they loved one another. It was a little house and the walls were thin. And following those nights when he heard their bed squeaking, nothing seemed different between them the next morning.

Tom's black eyes and short black hair complimented his demeanor. He was a little over six feet and heavy set. His voice generally matched his size. "I sure as hell hope you two ain't very hungry cuz I could eat the butt out of a dead skunk." He then laughed at his own tired joke. Teddy felt obliged to laugh along.

Agnes timed the pouring of Tom's coffee with his sitting down at the head of their small table. She barely pulled the spout away when he picked up the steaming cup and took a noisy sip. Instantly, he pulled his mouth away and dashed his head to the side. "That damned sure is hot."

Agnes had just finished pouring herself some coffee when Tom said to her, "You wanna fetch me the Crow. I believe I'm gonna need a little extra something to thaw my innards."

Teddy frowned before he could catch himself. Tom picked up on it and turned on him. "You little pecker neck. You'd be well advised to not be making faces in my direction or I'll smack it right off."

Agnes cut in as she turned back from the cupboard with the bottle of Old Crow in her hand. "There's no need to be calling Teddy vulgar names."

Tom jerked the bottle from her hand. "No need for him to be pulling faces, especially when he's about to eat my food."

Agnes wanted to fire back at Tom and tell him that she cooked and cleaned and washed his clothes and that she pulled her weight. But she knew in Tom's world those things didn't count for much. To him she wasn't much more than a piece of ass. To him she was replaceable. She sighed and turned away. "Let's just eat."

Tom uncapped the bottle and applied a generous pour to his coffee. He then laughed sarcastically and looked at Agnes who had sat down at the table katy-corner to him. He gestured with the bottle, "You want a splash a Crow?"

At that moment Teddy's eyes begged his mother to not lower herself to Tom's level. For a brief moment he fantasized that she had recognized his plea, but they both knew Tom would take it as an insult if she refused to drink with him and then supper would really go to hell.

Agnes slid her cup towards Tom. "Just a little."

Ignoring her, he tilted the bottle heavily bringing the level of coffee to the very brim of the cup. Agnes couldn't help herself. "Dammit, Tom. That's too much."

He laughed arrogantly. "Drink it. It'll dull the pain of life."

His words, *the pain of life*, echoed in her mind. It occurred to her he was verbalizing what he felt, or for that matter, how they all felt about their existence. She knew better than to go there. Instead, she took a sip of her coffee and grimaced slightly. "Doing the dishes after this will be interesting."

Tom started to laugh, but then abruptly stopped and looked at Teddy who had just speared a slice of roast. "Your boy here can do the dishes. He ain't done nuthin' else today,"

"That's not so, Tom. He-"

"It's alright, Ma. I'll do the dishes."

Tom piled on. "And when you're done with that shovel a path to the front door. It ain't nuthin' now but hardpacked ruts. Be easy enough for a person to slip and bust their ass."

Teddy set his fork down. He said, in a deliberately calm voice, "You got a shovel?"

"There's a scoop shovel in the back of my truck."

Teddy put his hands on the red and white checkered oilcloth and pushed his chair back from the table.

"Tom, it's dark. Can't this wait until he gets home from school tomorrow?"

"It's ok, Ma. I'd just as soon get it done now." And with that Teddy got up and headed for the coat rack by the door.

Agnes glared at Tom. "Are ya happy?"

He shot back. "Don't get a smart mouth with me, bitch."

Teddy suddenly appeared in the entry to the kitchen. He seethed the words in a tone like he was capable of dealing with what might result. "Don't you be calling my mother names."

Tom sneered at him. "Or what? She is a bitch."

It was more impulse than courage that caused Teddy to lunge at Tom. Just before things went dark, he thought he heard his mother scream.

CHAPTER FOUR

They had all of their stuff in the back of Jess Whitworth's pickup. It was bitterly cold outside. They were bundled up, Jess, Teddy and Agnes. Even though Jess had the heater on high Agnes still felt chilled. She wondered if it was truly the cold, as it had snowed another six inches last night, or if it was fear of what awaited her that caused these involuntary shivers.

The cab had grown uncomfortably quiet, save for the clanking of the tire chains on the rear wheels, when Jess said again, "George Phillips is a good man. I think you'll like working for him."

Agnes looked over at Jess. He appeared almost like a cartoon character with his rosy cheeks and clean-shaven face protruding from beneath his red cap and turned down ear flaps. His hands, encased in fuzzy green cloth gloves, had a two-hand grip on the steering wheel. He guided the pickup through the deep snow with the same confidence he'd had coming to their house last night and putting Tom in his place. It wasn't a physical confrontation, but rather it was a situation where Tom had held on to just enough of his common sense to realize that without his job he'd be out in the cold. In his entire 45 years of living all he had to show for it was his pickup that the bank held a note on, a couple of guns, and his clothes. And if he pissed off Jess, he might not even have those things. Agnes said, "I appreciate your helping us out, Mr. Whitworth."

"Well, sure, sure. Something had to change before one of you killed the other."

She came back, the epitome of meekness, 'I'm sorry for the bother."

"No need. Tom would be a hard man to live with."

Teddy scoffed, "You can say that again."

Jess asked, like he already knew, "You and Tom didn't get along?"

Teddy and Jess sat shoulder to shoulder, about equal in size. Teddy, however, with his blue stocking hat pulled down over his ears and just above his eyebrows looked to be the kid he was. His appearance did not bode well for him when he said, "No, but I'm gonna join the Navy."

Jess looked over, seemingly studying the blonde peach fuzz on Teddy's face. "How old are you?"

Teddy hesitated, like lying was an option.

Agnes cut in. "He's 15 and he's not joining the Navy."

"But Ma-"

Jess interrupted, "It's a moot point. You gotta be at least 17, even if your mother signs for you."

Agnes glared at Teddy. "So, you were expecting me to lie about your age."

"Lots of guys are doing it."

"You can get in trouble for doing that," said Jess.

Agnes sighed. "And I don't need any more trouble in my life."

Teddy blurted out, "Well, if you hadn't tied up with Tom we wouldn't be in this fix."

A sudden silence enveloped the cab. Nine or ten clanks of the tire chains went by before Jess waded into it. "We all make mistakes, Teddy. Maybe next time your Ma will pick a better man."

Anger tempered with shame surged through Agnes. She wanted to scream at both of them with all of the sarcasm that she could muster, *Oh yes, I'll be sure and do that next time.* She looked away momentarily lest they see the hurt they'd caused. It seemed that her life was just one hurt after another. She and Teddy had spent the night at Jess's house. His wife had fixed them supper since they hadn't been able to eat at their own place on account of the fight. After Jess and Tom had fed the cows this morning Jess had come for them and their stuff. He said Tom thought it would be for the best if her and Teddy moved out. Just like that, move out in the dead of winter. Not a note or a *I'm sorry it had to be this way* or *kiss my ass.* Kind of like telling a stray dog to *just git.*

It was about ten miles from Jess's place to the Phillips ranch. The last five were in silence with the three of them looking mostly straight ahead through the frost-free openings that the struggling defroster had cleared. Rolling sagebrush hills with pine filled draws and north slopes dominated the terrain. A blanket of ashen clouds dulled the brilliance of the new snow and added to their somber mood. At last, the gravel road topped a ridge and dropped down to a wooden bridge spanning Icehouse Creek. Aspen and willows lined its banks. The chained wheels rattled the planks as the truck crossed over the bridge. Directly ahead was a barbed wire fence with a cattleguard. Jess stopped the truck short of the metal grate eyeing it and the wire gate next to it. "Don't know that it'd be a smart thing to do, going across that cattleguard with chains on."

To her credit, Agnes opened her door and started to slide off the seat. "I'll open the gate."

"You sure," said Jess looking at the tautness of the wire loop that held the wooden dancer in the gate to the larger fence post. "Some of these can take two men and a boy to open."

Agnes smiled politely. "I'll give it a try."

Jess backed his truck up and pulled off the main road so as to align with the gate as Agnes trudged through the snow that was near the tops of her cowboy boots. Her breath pulsed in little white clouds in the biting air and her heart was pounding not from exertion but fear that she wouldn't be strong enough to open the gate. She wanted badly to prove herself in this man's world. Stepping next to the gate she could tell right away that it wasn't going to be easy. She'd opened gates before when she'd rode along with Tom on Mr. Whitworth's place. But those gates, upright and kind of lazy and weak, still served their purpose even though she had sufficient upper body strength to open them. On her first attempt she gripped the wooden dancer and pushed with her upper body as hard as she could towards the fence post, but the wire loop holding the gate up didn't budge. She was on her second attempt when she heard a vehicle behind her that soon rumbled over the cattleguard and stopped. A big man with a red bushy moustache wearing a black felt hat, that looked like something a miner would wear, got out of an old blue Ford truck. He started towards Agnes with a black and white sheep dog following him. The dog reached Agnes first. He was barking excitedly. Agnes knew to just stand still.

The man shouted, "That's enough, Wolf." And then he said, looking at Agnes, "You must be the new cook."

The man's demeanor, especially his green eyes, appeared kind to Agnes. She responded, "I am."

And then he looked beyond her at the sounds of pickup doors closing. "Hey Jess, did you bring all this damned snow with you?"

Jess laughed. "You'll thank me next summer."

George Phillips grunted slightly as he opened the gate. Agnes took note of his effort and grinned slightly.

Jess came next to them. He said to George, "I see you've met Agnes. This is her son, Teddy."

Phillips nodded. "So, you wanna come cook for my lambing crew."

Agnes suspected that Jess had told Phillips of her situation, she replied simply, "Yes, if you're hiring I do."

"Pays $200 a month and found if that suits ya."

Agnes glanced toward Teddy. "And my son?"

"He go to school?"

"He does."

"I'll expect him to work weekends for his keep."

The first thing that popped into Teddy's mind was to say, *I'm joining the Navy, so I won't be here long.* But then the reality of what Jess had said on the ride over smothered that. He said aloud in a positive tone that caused his mother to flash a smile of relief, "I'd be happy to do whatever needs done, Sir."

Phillips looked from Agnes to Teddy. "Be mostly hauling hay and feeding and watering sheep." He paused while looking Teddy over. "How much do you weigh?"

Teddy gave himself an extra five pounds. "135, Sir."

Phillips smiled while gently bobbing his head with approval or skepticism, Teddy wasn't certain which it was, before saying, "I make a stout bale. Wire tie. They'll run 75-80 pounds."

Teddy came back quick, even though the bales at Jess's that he'd occasionally had to help Tom with were string tie and about 20 pounds lighter. "Not a problem, Sir."

Phillips laughed. "Well, I'd advise you to have a coupla extra of your Ma's flapjacks on the days you wrestle these bales."

"Yes, Sir."

And then the husky sheepman, standing at least a head taller than Teddy, hesitated while looking him in the eye, he said, "This ain't the Army, son. My name's George."

Since he felt mostly responsible for their last situation blowing up, he was trying extra hard to make this one work.

To that end the words escaped him, "Yes sir – I mean ok, George."

Everyone laughed but Teddy.

They continued on up the narrow dirt road that lay beneath a foot of snow. George led the way. He was not chained up but did have a load of hay on that seemed to give him good traction. It was close to a half mile through a pasture with scattered Ponderosa pine trees to the ranch headquarters in the mouth of a big canyon. A little creek called Red Rock bounded by more aspen and willows and some pines flowed out of the canyon. It stayed to the south of the ranch buildings and angled down across the pasture to join up with Icehouse Creek.

"Quite an outfit," said Jess as they bounced along behind George.

Agnes and Teddy were impressed. To the north of them was a vast expanse of pens, half sheds facing south, and canvas covered sheds with stovepipes on each end. Blue smoke coiled up from each of the rusty tin pipes. And sheep, all of the pens had ewes and lambs in them. Agnes looked over at Jess. "It must have taken a long time to acquire all of this."

Jess turned left just short of a thicket of Ponderosa pine that partially concealed a big log house with a large, roofed porch and sitting chairs. He glanced over at Agnes. "George's grandpa settled here in 1876."

"Same year as Custer got massacred," offered Teddy.

Jess dashed his head to the side for emphasis. "Back then this country wasn't for sissies."

"It still isn't," said Agnes.

Up ahead George had parked in front of an old log building with a dirt roof. The logs had weathered to a dull gray. Agnes wondered if George's grandfather had built it.

Jess parked beside George's pickup. He grinned in a good way. "Home sweet home."

He'd not purposely conjured it up but the thought played in Teddy's mind, *at least Ma isn't having to sleep with somebody she doesn't care about to get this place.*

George said as they drew near, "Ain't had a cook for over a week. Last one went on a bender in Bozeman and got his self locked up."

"Well, where do your men eat?" asked Agnes.

"They're batchin' it."

A puzzled look came to her face.

George pointed beyond her. "See those sheep camps parked over there and that old trailer down by the crik. That's where these fellas live. So right now, I'm buying groceries for four different cooks that are whining about having to eat their own cooking. When they're out in the mountains with the sheep they have to cook for themselves." He paused and laughed. "I guess now they think they're entitled to be pampered."

Agnes barely heard what Phillips had said as her attention had gone to the shack that was to be her and Teddy's new home. It didn't appear to have a yard of any kind as there was no fence surrounding it, just lots of undisturbed creamy white snow. There were four-pane windows that lacked curtains to either side of the door which was plain except for its white doorknob. A rusty stovepipe protruded from the roof. It was definitely a step down from what they'd had to leave. Agnes' mind went back to last night. *Damned Tom. Why'd he have to be such a jerk?*

Oblivious to where Agnes' was at, George pointed to the woodshed and outhouse next to it about a hundred feet to the right of the cabin. "Got a sink and running water for cooking but never got around to installing a toilet or bathtub."

Agnes' disappointment that bordered on anger bled through to her eyes. George picked up on it. "There's a nice sized metal bathtub in your room. You can heat water on the stove. That's what ole Shorty did." He paused and laughed.

"Except he didn't do it often enough." Phillips laughed again. Jess chimed in too while Agnes and Teddy barely cracked a grin. It struck them, or at least Agnes it did, that they were going the wrong direction in life.

George started toward the cabin door calling over his shoulder, "Well, let's get you situated." Snow had blown up against the door such that when he opened it a minor avalanche slid onto the wood floor. George stepped inside as did the others. "Here's the cookin' and eatin' area," he announced, as if they couldn't see that. A rectangular wooden table with six wooden chairs around it filled much of the room. Permanently clustered in the center of the table were salt and pepper shakers, a sugar bowl, ketchup and Tabasco sauce. Beyond the table was a stove, wood box, counter and cupboards. To their right, beneath another four-pane window, was a white porcelain sink. Next to it was a white refrigerator. On the opposite end of the room against the log wall was an old pale green couch. On the wall above it, hanging from an over-size nail, was a Winchester Firearms calendar for the year 1941. A half dozen ten penny nails for the purpose of hanging coats and hats had been driven into the wall at eye level to the left of the door. A tattered green mackinaw hung from one of the nails. But, as much as anything, the room was defined by the white chinking between the logs.

After a brief time of silent observation, George turned towards the door to the left of the couch like all that was in the kitchen was self-explanatory. "Back here," he said opening the door, are your quarters.

Within seconds Agnes had taken it all in. It was spartan, but not so much that it shocked her as she had lived in some dumps during her life. There was a single brass bed, a wooden chair next to it with a wind-up alarm clock that had run down, a three-tier dresser with no mirror and, beneath the window to their left, a brass bathtub. A doorless closet, about two feet wide, was located in the corner of the room near the head of the bed. Clothes were hanging in it. Agnes assumed they belonged to the man who was in the Bozeman jail. She said, trying to sound positive, "Teddy, I guess you'll sleep on the couch."

Teddy nodded while thinking, *until I join the Navy, I will.*

Agnes turned to George. "When do I start?"

"Breakfast tomorrow."

"I guess I should take stock of what food is here."

George registered mild embarrassment. "I hadn't thought of that." He paused thoughtfully and then said with some reluctance, "Hopefully we won't have to go to town for groceries, at least not today."

Agnes knew the situation. It was close to one o'clock and twenty-three miles to town. The January sun was down by six o'clock. She said, her breath hanging in the frigid air, "I'll try to make do."

Phillips' demeanor brightened. "Alright then, let's get your stuff moved in."

Bringing their belongings in was an awkward moment for all of them. Three suitcases and two cardboard boxes was all there was. Not even enough for everybody to feel useful. Thirty-seven years of living. This, and a broke down car was all Agnes had to show for it.

CHAPTER FIVE

Neither George or Jess lingered after Agnes and Teddy's belongings were inside. George had said, *I'll be back by later to check on you,* while Jess assured her, *in the spring we'll tow your car over here.* He said nothing about fixing it. As she watched him drive away, she became fearful. She wondered if when Jess got home Tom would inquire how things went. For a moment she even fantasized that he'd be regretful and sorry how it had turned out between them.

And then Teddy said, "I should build a fire, don't you think?"

Agnes sniffed and dabbed at her runny nose with her gloved hand. "Yes, it's miserably cold in here."

Teddy laughed. "Good sleeping weather, huh?"

Agnes scoffed. "Yeah, you could go to sleep and never wake up."

An inspection of the refrigerator revealed a plate of butter, a large bowl of eggs, a pitcher of milk that had soured and some leftover beef stew that probably should be thrown out as well. The cupboards were still fairly well stocked with canned goods, flour, sugar, cold cereal, spam, and a large sack of pinto beans. In short supply, however, was coffee, syrup, ketchup, mustard, salt, oatmeal and fresh meat.

Teddy had a fire going. It popped in response to some pitchy wood. He looked at his mother who was pouring the bad milk down the sink. "Well, are we gonna starve?"

"Not for a day or two."

Teddy knew better than to say it, but he couldn't help himself. "I've heard they feed you pretty good in the Navy."

Agnes frowned. "You also heard what Jess said."

"They'd believe you if you told them I was seventeen."

"Maybe, but that's not going to happen."

"But Ma, I'm missing the war."

Agnes finished rinsing the empty milk pitcher and then set it in the sink before pausing to look at him. "You think this is just going to be some fun adventure, Teddy?"

"It's the patriotic thing to do."

"If you were older you'd have my blessing. I wouldn't like it, but I'd support you."

"The war will be over by the time I'm old enough to join."

"Does there have to be a war going on for you to enlist?"

Teddy's frustration boiled over. He spit the words at her, "You just don't want to live here in this crap hole by yourself."

Agnes' eyes got watery. She fought the urge to full-on cry. "It wouldn't bother you leaving me here alone?"

Teddy felt bad. He regretted it had come to this. "I got my own life to live, Ma. Besides sooner or later another man will come into your life and chances are I'll be a nuisance just like with Tom."

Agnes thought to disagree, but the fight last night and the fact that they were now in this log shack made that seem foolish. Tears started to overflow her eyelids causing Teddy to step towards her. She put up her hand. "No, Teddy, let me think about this." And with that she pulled a pack of cigarettes from her coat pocket. She was slow and methodical, like she was already thinking, in shaking one out far enough to clasp it with her lips before lighting it with a match struck on the stove. Her cheeks caved in as she drew heavily on the cigarette and then expelled the smoke. Teddy stood quiet, absorbing the smell of tobacco and the residual smells of cooking. She said, like she'd forgotten what they were talking about, "Don't let me forget, I need to make a list of what we need."

Teddy nodded, "Alright."

And then she said, "You know, I'd just as soon be dead than live without you."

Teddy frowned. "Oh, Ma."

"It's true, Teddy."

"It'll be ok. You'll see."

Agnes stepped to the table and flicked the ash from her cigarette into an ashtray next to the ketchup bottle. She then took another long draw, squinting her left eye as she did. She said, "I guess we'll see."

Teddy's demeanor brightened. "So, you'll sign for me?"

"You mean lie for you?"

"I guess so."

Agnes took another draw on her cigarette like she didn't know what to do next. She could see the excited look in Teddy's eyes. He was damned near giddy. She, on the other hand, felt alone and unwanted. Not by Tom, not by any good man and now her own son. Her mind picked the words carefully. "Alright Teddy, your happiness in exchange for mine. Helluva deal, don't you think?"

Teddy flashed a hurt look that wasn't very convincing. His mind was already out of the cold Montana winter and in the warmth of San Diego and the Navy's boot camp. "Oh Ma, I'm sorry."

Agnes ignored his apology and started for the door. She said, without looking at him, "There's a root cellar south of the cook shack. I'm gonna go check it."

"I can do that, Ma."

Her tone was abrupt. "You can fill the wood box." Before he could respond the door had closed behind her.

CHAPTER SIX

For supper, they split a can of chili and a can of peaches along with some dry crackers and coffee. The air between them was a potpourri of emotions, mostly none of them good. There was no more talk about the Navy but then Agnes, knowingly or not, offered up a nexus to it. "So, what about school? You going tomorrow?"

George had told them the bus came by the turn to the ranch around 6:45 but wouldn't know to come down to the house and probably never would until the snow melted. Teddy frowned. "If I'm going into the Navy, I don't see the point."

Agnes came back in an arbitrary tone. "I have no idea when we can get you signed up. I've got a job and besides that, I'm afoot. So, in the meantime, you might as well be going to school."

Before he thought how it would sound, he said, "I'd have to walk to the bus stop in the dark and the snow's up to my knees." Regret instantly consumed him.

Agnes pounced on his words. She laughed sarcastically. "And you want to go in the Navy?"

For a moment he felt helpless to respond, but then it occurred to him that maybe he could get the Navy form while he was in town for school and bring it home. He said, letting his mother think she'd shamed him into going to school,

"You're probably right, Ma. I should go to school until I get joined up."

Agnes pushed her chair back from the table and stood. "A little more schooling couldn't hurt you."

Teddy looked at his mother, while in his mind he saw himself going to the recruiter's office tomorrow. "You're right, Ma. Smarts is something a fella can never get too much of."

She allowed herself a weak smile, her mood slightly better than when supper had begun. She didn't belabor her minor victory but put on her coat saying, "I'm going to the privy."

The snow crunched beneath her feet. Already her cheeks stung from the cold night air. It had been an effort to not complain in front of Teddy about having to go to the outhouse in these conditions. Instead, in her mind she cursed Tom for ruining the life they had.

The root cellar contained food, staples necessary to feed four men and herself. The back part of it was an icehouse filled with meat while the outer, less cold part, held spuds, carrots, onions and beets that George had harvested from his garden. *It plum just slipped my mind*, he'd said in reference to the cellar when he stopped by about sundown.

Agnes wanted to make a good impression. In the morning she would have ham, eggs, diced spuds with onions, hotcakes and coffee. She wound the clock and set the alarm for four-thirty. It was now 8:15p.m.. Breakfast was to be at six. She undressed in the dark on account of there being no curtains on the windows in her room. Straight out from the cook shack about a hundred yards or so was a couple of the sheep camps. A dull yellow glow was evident through their white canvas tops. In the moonlight she could see blue smoke trailing up from each camp's stovepipe. Its silhouette reminded her of a postcard she'd seen one time. She imagined the men in the camps were warmer than she was. She had no heat except what came from the stove in the kitchen through her open door. Sleep was hard to come by. Her bedding smelled of sour sweat. Tomorrow, in between preparing three meals, she would wash it assuming there was soap. A wash board leaned against the wall next to the bathtub. She supposed the tub was used for clothes too. And then, close to ten, she heard voices over by the sheep camps. Boredom over-rode the cold. Wearing only her flannel shirt and long underwear she went to the window. In the moonlight she could see two men relieving themselves in front of the nearest sheep wagon. They were talking in loud irresponsible voices, drunk talk, she thought. She watched them until they had finished and gone back inside. Her room was cold. She shivered, her nipples hardened. The stove's popping and cracking had been replaced by Teddy's heavy rhythmic breathing. The kind that made a mother feel good. She'd barely gotten back in bed when the urge to pee hit her. In her mind she cursed the drunker sheepherders for bringing it on. And then she cursed the fact she was a woman and didn't have the convenience they had. In the end she cursed Tom for putting her here.

A little past midnight she succumbed to the discomfort, got dressed and went outside. The intense cold immediately gripped her such that her teeth chattered. The herders' camps were dark and quiet prompting her to consider doing as they had right there to the side of the door. She took a couple of steps in that direction even reaching to unbuckle her belt before the image of her tracks leading to yellow snow and the men laughing flooded her mind. She turned, the shivering emanating from deep within her chest was near painful and started towards the privy. *And to think I gave Teddy grief about walking to the bus.* A maze of stars twinkled overhead, their brightness second only to the moon. Inside the outhouse, however, the darkness could be cut with a knife. Agnes pushed the door open so as to be able to see the toilet paper and dropped her pants. The relief she had anticipated was overshadowed by her buttocks coming in contact with the frigid wood. She was nearly done when she heard a vehicle. Stepping outside she saw its headlights coming from the direction of the sheep sheds. She was midway between the privy and the cook shack when the lights illuminated her. She stopped and briefly looked into them before going on, her breath huffing out in the night air like a cartoon dragon. The lights turned and went on disappearing into the trees where George lived. Agnes whispered, "I hope he feels guilty." But then she recalled agreeing with Jess that this was, *no country for sissies.*

CHAPTER SEVEN

Agnes felt in the dark for the box of stick matches on the chair beside her bed, selected one and brought it to life near the face of the alarm clock. She sighed, *five past four. 25 minutes till the alarm goes off.* She wagged the match out before it burned her fingers and dropped it with the others which now totaled five. Only one of them had been for her bedtime smoke, the others marked her insomnia throughout the night to read the clock. It wasn't just that she was chilled and uncomfortable in a bed that smelled of an unclean man. It was more than that. She'd cooked for men before. There'd been the mine where she'd met Teddy's father and several ranches after that. But today, this was different. It had to be right and good. She had no place to go if it wasn't.

By ten till six she had enough bacon fried and in the warming oven so that each person could have four slices. And the spuds were done too. Steam was rolling out the open top of a black metal coffee pot sitting to one side of the stove. And hotcake batter, a huge white bowl of it, sat on the counter. She was ready for them. Her confidence was such that the worry knots in her stomach had started to unravel, just a little.

Sensing his mother's apprehension, Teddy said, "Smells real good, Ma."

Agnes looked up from how Teddy had set the table. She breathed through her nose in an exaggerated way. The smell of bacon and coffee permeated the warm air. She allowed herself to smile. "It does, doesn't it."

Abruptly, their eyes shifted to the door. Voices and the stomping of feet sounded outside. Laughter and the door opened. Two men and a blast of cold air came inside. Spontaneous "good-mornings" walked over one another so as to render them superfluous. With a potholder, Agnes picked up the big coffee pot while the men hung their hats and coats. She did not ask the obvious but poured coffee in the cups where they intended to sit. She said, before returning the pot to the stove, "My name's Agnes Kinney." Nodding to her right where Teddy was sitting, she added, "and this is my son, Teddy."

The men glanced in Teddy's direction. It was apparent to Agnes that the bigger of the two, who was older and mostly gray haired was about to offer up his name when right out of the chute, it began. His partner, smaller, bald-headed, clean shaven with a white tee shirt visible at the neck of his tan work shirt blurted out, like he would be making points with the new cook, "Well, you ain't Tom Kinney's wife, are ya?"

Agnes came back quick, lest her discomfort rise to the surface. "Yes, I am." She turned away to set the coffee on the stove.

The little man said to her back, "That ole Tom is a good hand. He sure enough is." He paused briefly and then threw out the obvious. "So, how is it you're here cookin'?"

Ignoring the question Agnes removed the bacon and diced spuds from the oven and set them on the table. She then looked at the men like Tom's name had never been spoken and addressed them as if she was a stern schoolmarm, "And what do I call you gentlemen?"

The little man's expectant green eyes hinted embarrassment at his apparent social gaff. He responded quickly, "Name's Eddy Parsons, Ma'am."

Shifting her eyes to the big man, he said, "Fred Anderson, Ma'am."

Agnes went on, crowding Eddy's white elephant into a corner of the room, hoping that it would just go away. "How many eggs you fellas want?"

"Two," said Eddy. "And you can flip 'em over once."

"Same for me," said Fred.

A blue and green gallon size tin bucket of Morrell lard sat on the end of the counter near the stove. With her metal spatula, Agnes scooped a glob of lard and dropped it into a cast iron skillet on the stove. It immediately began to sizzle and pop. As she cracked the eggs into the pan, she called over her shoulder, "How many hotcakes do ya want?"

"Depends on how big they are," said Eddy.

"I'll make 'em as big as you want."

"Alright, I'll take a couple just short of covering the plate."

"I'll take the same," said Fred.

"Coming up."

Agnes was ladling the hotcake batter onto the griddle portion of the stove when she heard a vehicle outside. Momentarily the headlights flooded through the window by the door followed by the engine cutting off and doors closing.

"Coupla more customers for ya," said Billy in a loud voice.

"That's fine," said Agnes as she carefully gaged the size of the puddles of batter. The voices outside grew louder and, in that instant before the door opened, Agnes recognized one of them. Her heart tripped over itself as a flood of adrenaline consumed her. *Oh no, it can't be.* And then the door opened to a boisterous man and another less so. Agnes did not speak nor turn around but turned the eggs instead. In thirty seconds they would be done and she would have to face the men.

The loud man boomed, "Now what's that they say about the first hogs to the trough being the first ones to slaughter?"

Eddy scoffed. "Shit, Pete, you just can't roll your sorry ass out in the morning. And poor Frank there, since he rides to breakfast with ya he's stuck waiting until you've had your beauty sleep."

Pete laughed. "Well, at least it's doing me some good. In your case, Eddy, you could sleep for a week straight and it wouldn't help."

All four of the hired men and Teddy laughed suggesting that Pete had won out in the bantering. And then Agnes turned around with the eggs on a plate.

A shocked look came to Pete's face before he roared, "Well, I'll be go to hell. It's a small world."

All eyes shifted to Agnes. The most surprised among them was Teddy. It was as quiet as a dead man in the room. It was like Agnes had become the main attraction and they'd all bought a ticket to hear what she had to say. Her voice was quivery. "Hello, Pete. I didn't know you were in the country."

He laughed loudly and then said with no apparent shame, "Well, I been a guest of the state over at Deerlodge. Just checked outta there about a month ago."

Agnes turned away and began flipping the hotcakes.

Pete looked at Teddy. He said in a loud voice, as he generally said everything, "This your boy?"

Agnes kept her attention on the hotcakes. "Yes, his name is Teddy."

Pete was seated at the end of the table opposite Teddy. He laughed again and looked straight at him. "Son, I'm the black sheep of the Walker family. I'm your Uncle Pete."

Teddy appeared uneasy. What little his mother had told him about his uncle had been bad. She'd said, *he's a shiftless drunken criminal and not worth talking about.* Those words played in Teddy's head as he looked at his uncle. "Pleased to meet you, Sir."

Pete laughed. "I like you already. Nobody ever calls me sir."

Teddy offered a silent manufactured grin.

"So, how old are you?"

"Fifteen. Gonna be sixteen pretty soon."

Pete took some bacon and passed the plate to Frank. "So, when's your birthday?"

With her back to the table, Agnes said in a loud voice, "It doesn't matter, Pete." She then pivoted quickly from the stove with two hotcakes balanced on a spatula and extended them to Eddy and Fred.

Pete said with a phony smile and some edge in his voice, "Why's that?"

Agnes turned to the stove, her mind having gone back in time. *Why does this sonovabitch have to show up now and ruin what little I've got going here.* She scooped more lard and began ladling hotcake batter.

Pete came again, his tone bordering on anger. "Tell me, Agnes, why doesn't it matter? Hell, I was thinkin' I'd get the boy a present."

Agnes cracked some eggs in the skillet mindful of the fact that her differences with Pete couldn't interfere with feeding the other men. She said, mostly to Frank, "How do you like your eggs?"

He looked at Pete, who was still staring at Agnes' back, and then stammered like he was sorry to interrupt, "Scrambled is fine."

Teddy broke the tension. "It's May 17th."

Pete smiled like he'd won out and looked at Teddy. "I knew it was in the spring. It had to be. I just couldn't place the date."

Agnes turned the hotcakes. It was difficult to keep her focus. Her inner self wanted to scream at Pete to stop the game of cat and mouse.

And then he pushed his luck thinking, or perhaps knowing, that he held the high ground. He said in a loud voice to

Agnes' back, "What the hell does a fella have to do to get a hotcake in this place?"

Agnes kept quiet. Seconds later she stood at the corner of the table between Pete and Frank with two steaming hotcakes on her spatula. Frank took one. "Thank you, Ma'am." Pete took the other, but said nothing.

For a time they ate mostly in silence, Pete having caused an uneasiness in the room. Everyone seemed guarded in what they said, or they just didn't talk. People were nearly done eating.

On the wall behind Teddy, to the right of the calendar, was a saucer sized black clock with a white face. It was the fourth time that he'd looked around to check the time. It was 6:28. He slid his chair back and started for the coat rack.

"You going somewhere?" said Pete.

"Gotta catch the school bus."

Pete snorted. "It's colder 'n a well-digger's ass out there, don't ya know?"

Teddy nodded, but said nothing, as he pulled his blue stocking cap down over his disheveled blonde hair.

"You wanna ride?"

"No Sir, I believe I'm good."

Pete glanced at Agnes and shook his head before coming back to Teddy. "Alright, you have yourself a nice hike."

From the corner of his eye Teddy could see his mother. He wanted to believe that it would have been ok for him to accept the ride, but her eyes said otherwise. And then he knew that he'd read her right when she came around the table and gave him a hug. It made him feel uncomfortable as he knew it was for show.

CHAPTER EIGHT

In spite of the tension between Pete and his mother Teddy half expected Pete to come and give him a ride to the bus stop, but he did not. The bus, the same one that he would have gotten on at about ten past seven had he still been living at the Whitworth ranch, went on by him by a couple hundred yards or so before the brake lights came on. Teddy stood where he was for a few seconds until it became apparent to him that the bus wasn't going to back up in the dark and rutted snow. He began to jog hoping that old Marvin Jones wouldn't begin to second guess himself and question if he hadn't seen a deer instead of a person. It seemed like a long way to Teddy in his cowboy boots and overshoes. By the time he got to the bus, the cold air had his lungs burning and his eyes watering. Marvin folded the door open. He paused in his humming. "'Bout missed ya."

Still catching his breath, Teddy said, "Yeah, we moved."

"Oh. " Marvin snapped the door shut and resumed his humming as he ground the old Chevy bus into second gear and urged it forward. With the exception of the seat right behind Marvin, which was occupied by the Miller sisters, ages eight and ten, Teddy had his pick of where to sit. He wobbled down the aisle a couple more rows before taking a seat on the side of the bus opposite the Miller girls and slid over next to the window. It was a world of darkness and cold, both outside and inside the bus. Marvin lived at the head of the valley, about three miles beyond George Phillips' ranch, near the mouth of Whiskey Creek. He took the bus home at night after dropping the Millers off just a half mile down from his place. Teddy had not considered how cold the bus would still be three rows back from the heater near Marvin, but his mind was elsewhere. Leaning forward he folded his arms across the top of the seat in front of him and rested his forehead. It was quiet save for the gentle whining of the old bus's transmission. Occasionally his head would bounce. Most days he could sleep through it. Today was different. Pete was center stage in his mind and to the side of him was his mother's hateful look. The friction between them gnawed at Teddy. *She's gonna turn the others against her, against the both of us. They'll side with Pete. Don't know why she has to be so hardnosed.* The bus began to slow down. Teddy looked up. They were coming to the Polson ranch. In the headlights he could see his best friend Jimmy and his little brother, Eric, standing by the side of the road. Beyond them was a green clapboard house sitting amongst pine trees with a white picket fence surrounding all of it. The lights were on. A picture window facing the road allowed Teddy to see inside right through the living room into the kitchen. Mrs. Polson was washing dishes. She was a pretty woman who went to church and didn't smoke or drink or swear. Teddy had gone to Jimmy's 17th birthday party not long ago. It was a nice house. He was envious.

The door flopped open and the Polson boys came stomping on the bus, not wanting the snow to cling to their boots any longer than necessary. Ten year old Eric sat behind the Miller girls so that he could pester them. Jimmy moved on as the bus began to rock. And then he called out in surprise, "What are you doing on here so early?"

"We moved."

Jimmy dropped into the seat next to Teddy. "Wow, when did this happen?"

"Yesterday."

"So'd Tom get a job somewhere else?"

"No. my mother did."

Jimmy paused as if to process the meaning of this.

Teddy added, "She's cookin' for George Phillips' hired men."

"Oh, yeah, I heard Slim got tanked up in Bozeman and got his self thrown in the hoosgow."

Teddy was embarrassed. He hated being who he was. Jimmy knew the old cook, so he likely knew where they were living. He put it out there. Just to get it over with. "We're living in the cook shack."

Jimmy was slow in responding. "How's that?"

"Not good."

Jimmy's curiosity kicked in. "And your dad, he didn't go?"

"He ain't my dad."

"Sorry."

"No, me and Tom had differences. My mom got in the middle of it and then everything just went to hell."

"That's too bad."

Teddy shook his head. "Yeah, and guess who's working for Mr. Phillips. My no account uncle."

"Pete Walker is your uncle?"

Teddy snorted, mildly surprised. "You know him?"

Jimmy hesitated before saying in a guarded tone, "Not personally."

"Well then, how do you know him?"

Jimmy sighed. "I don't know that I should say. It's kinda personal."

Teddy shot back in a sharp tone saying the words one by one, "What do you mean, personal?"

Jimmy looked up to make sure that his brother was still preoccupied with the Miller girls and then facing Teddy, lowered his voice. "A coupla weeks ago my mother got stuck.

Pete stopped to help and ended up getting pretty fresh with her. I guess she slapped him and he shoved her. About then a car came along so he left. When Mom got home she told my dad and he went looking for Pete. I guess he told him that he'd kill him if he ever went near my mom again."

"What'd Pete do?"

"Tried to say my mom was coming on to him. I don't think my dad believed him, but it still caused him and my mother to have words."

"They say all this stuff in front of you?"

"No, I was in my room with the door open and they thought I was outside with Eric."

"Oh."

"They don't know that I heard them. I'd appreciate it if you'd keep this to yourself."

Teddy was feeling some shame that it was his uncle, a Walker, who had brought this unsavoriness into his best friend's life. He said to himself, *more trashy Walker doings*. His mind flashed back to when he was seven years old, and they lived in a little Kansas town. His real dad worked at the grain elevator and after work was a regular at one or the other of two bars on the town's main street. The size of the town lent itself to everybody knowing what everybody else was doing, both good and bad. Unless you had it coming or the person saying it was just mean spirited, people didn't rub your nose in the bad things. Timmy Reynolds, being eleven and one of the big kids, qualified as mean-spirited. It was morning recess, near the swings, that he'd said to Teddy in front of some other "big kids", *your dad is the town drunk*. Just straight out, for no apparent reason, as if it was a fact that needed to be stated. The other kids laughed as Teddy stood there feeling helpless to refute what he knew was common knowledge. He now said to Jimmy, "Your secret's safe with me."

"I appreciate it. My dad would be mad if he knew I was sharing all this."

"Hey, I don't want this gettin' around anymore than you do. Pete's a jerk and my mom and I are related to him. I'd hate for Mr. Phillips to put us in the same boat as him."

"I don't think you have to worry about that," whispered Jimmy.

"Why is that?"

"My dad went to Phillips. Told him he was gonna talk to the sheriff about Pete. Phillips begged him not to. Said Pete was an ex-Marine. Won some medals in World War I over in France. Asked my dad to give him a break."

Teddy was both surprised and impressed to hear about Pete's service. He didn't strike Teddy as someone who would take orders. Nonetheless, hearing this restored a little pride in the Walker name. It came to him that he should be honest with Jimmy and tell him about Pete being an ex-con. Instead, he said, "Your dad gonna call the sheriff?"

"I don't think so. Told Phillips he wouldn't."

Teddy supposed this was a good thing, but he wondered if Pete wouldn't screw it up. And then, like he'd reached his limit of gossip, he said, "You still thinkin' on joining up?"

"Yeah."

"The Marines?"

"Yeah, they'll take ya if you're 17 and your folks sign."

"You should come with me in the Navy."

"You're too young, Teddy. They ain't gonna let you in."

"I'm trying to get my mother to lie about my age."

Jimmy snorted. "Shit, Teddy, my mother would no more do that for me than a man in the moon."

"My situation is different."

Jimmy laughed. "Mothers are mothers."

Teddy recalled Jimmy's mother. Pretty, makeup, always dressed nice. And then Agnes, Levis, boots, a cigarette in the corner of her mouth and too often bloodshot eyes. He scoffed. "I don't think so."

Jimmy shook his head. "I'll still bet you a soda pop she won't do it."

Deep down, Teddy knew that Jimmy was probably right.

CHAPTER NINE

About a mile north of town the road turned to pavement mostly because a more well-traveled state highway from Billings intersected it. Marvin eased off the gas as he rolled past the "Entering Elkhorn – Pop. 1,083, sign". There were 27 kids on the bus. They would be delivered in two stops. Twelve of them at the elementary school on the east side of town and the rest at the junior/senior high school on the west side of town. After the elementary stop, the bus got noticeably quieter. Marvin then turned onto a side street, the same one that he always took going back to Main Street. It went through two blocks of old wood frame houses of varying colors, none of them bright or new, that were surrounded by cottonwood trees equal in age of the houses.

Main Street did not have the appearance of being especially prosperous. It was the usual assortment of businesses required to sustain a small town and the agricultural community surrounding it. The buildings reflected time, from a log cabin in need of staining that housed Ned's Barbershop, the oldest business on Main Street, to the newest, a tan brick building that Rexall Drug occupied. In between these architectural benchmarks were structures made of stone and wood and old brick. Some of them were two story, having apartments located above. It was these, or at least two of them, that held significance for Teddy. The first was the Lariat Bar.

When they had first come to town Agnes was in desperate need of work. After patronizing the Lariat for a short period of time, she was offered a job tending bar. It was early November when they moved into the apartment located directly above the bar room. She asked if she could work days so as to be home with Teddy at night but was told no, her being low person on the totem pole, so to speak. The memory of the night when the fallacy of this decision came to bear was never far from Teddy's mind's eye. The night, just a few days before Christmas, had begun like many others that he had come to resent. The music and drunken din came right up through the floor. It made it difficult for Teddy to listen to the radio or do his homework. On that night, when it all came to an end, he was laying on the couch where he normally slept. He was awake staring into the darkness listening for his mother's voice amongst all the others. He tried to make a game of putting faces to the voices. It was all imaginary though, as aside from his mother he knew only one other bar room voice and that was a man he'd actually met the week before. On that night there had been nothing in their apartment to eat except corn flakes, but there was no milk. Agnes had told him to never come down to the bar unless it was really important. Being as hungry as he was met that criteria, at least in Teddy's mind it did.

The stairs ended not far from the end of the bar. Teddy stood frozen on the bottom step. His courage had deserted him. The bar room was smokey and very crowded. A jukebox off to the left was playing and pool balls cracked on the table somewhere beyond the wall of bodies in front of Teddy. And then the bodies parted enough to where he caught a glimpse of his mother, standing behind the bar. She was leaning forward talking to a man sitting on the other side. The top two buttons of her red blouse were unbuttoned. The man appeared fixated on where they left off. Suddenly, she looked to her right at a man down the bar who was pointing at Teddy.

His lips were moving but Teddy couldn't hear what he said. It didn't matter as Agnes' head snapped around and she started towards him. There was a look of concern on her face but not one that would bode well for Teddy. She stopped directly in front of him and looked down. "You know you're not supposed to be here, don't you?"

His mother's eyes were glassy causing him to briefly regret coming, but then he went to it. "I was hopin' to get some money for a hamburger."

Agnes frowned at Teddy, unaware or not caring that a bearded man with a gray Stetson was watching. She said, in a stern voice, "Hells bells, Teddy. You know I ain't got no money."

Teddy glanced at the smoldering cigarette in his mother's hand. He knew there was a near new carton of Lucky Strikes upstairs. He knew too that they cost a lot more than a hamburger. He wanted to point that out to her, but he also knew it might get him slapped. He started to turn away when the bearded cowboy took a dollar bill off the bar in front of him and held it out to Teddy. "Here ya go, son."

Shamed, Agnes looked at the cowboy. "That ain't necessary, Mister. He's got things upstairs he can eat."

The man came back, his voice a deep southern drawl. "The boy's hungry, Ma'am."

For a few seconds, Agnes glared contemptuously at the man before walking off.

Teddy allowed her to take a few steps and then said to the man, "Thank you."

The cowboy smiled. "You're entirely welcome."

It wasn't until that night at the Lariat when Agnes tried to breakup a fight and got knocked out cold that Teddy heard the cowboy's voice again. This time, however, it was loud and angry shortly before everything just went to hell. Men were hollering, women screaming, profanity and threats filled the air. In the midst of it all he heard his mother shout

I'm callin' the cops, so you sons-ah-bitches better stop it right now. But they did not stop until the police came, and then it was too late. The hamburger cowboy lay dead on the floor by the pool table stabbed over a five dollar bet. Agnes went to the hospital to have her broken nose checked out. And Teddy dared not come down the stairs again.

In a few days, Agnes, black eyes, swollen nose and all, parted company with the Lariat and moved across the street to the Owl Café. And with that move came Tom Kinney.

They were coming up on the edge of town and the home of the Elkhorn Pirates, Marvin's next stop. It was a few minutes till eight. The sun was struggling to penetrate a bank of gray clouds that had parked itself on the mountains to the east. It's absence made the day feel even more somber to Teddy as he stepped off the bus into the churned up snow. He and Jimmy had just reached the sidewalk, which had been shoveled free of snow, when he stopped. Jimmy went on a few more steps before he realized that Teddy wasn't with him. He turned, "Whaddaya doin'?"

"I was thinkin' of going and seeing the recruiter."

"And cut class?"

Teddy frowned. "What's the difference? If I go in the Navy, I'll be gone anyway."

Jimmy sighed and shook his head. "I'm telling ya, Teddy, your chances of getting in the Navy are about zero."

Teddy looked towards town and then back at Jimmy. "If anybody asks tell 'em I had a doctor's appointment."

"You know you've got to check out at the office. And you've got to have a note from your mom."

"Just say the bus was late and I didn't have time."

"They'll ask Marvin."

"Maybe not." And then Teddy fell in with some junior high kids that were going to the white cinder block building next to the high school. They gave him funny looks until finally a dark haired girl with pigtails said, "I think you're going the wrong way."

Teddy smiled at the girl. "Not today, I'm not." He kept on walking. Within a minute or so he came to Main Street and turned right towards the courthouse where the recruiters maintained offices. There was a smattering of vehicles parked diagonally up and down the street. It was too early for some businesses like the Lariat or Mint bars to be open, but not the military. Right there in front of the courthouse was a blue-gray Chevy coupe with the words, US NAVY stenciled in black letters on the driver's door. Just the sight of it caused Teddy to briefly shiver inside. It was a feeling of both excitement and apprehension. What if the girl with pigtails had been right, *I think you're going the wrong way.*

Unlike the high school, the sidewalk leading to the courthouse steps was not shoveled. Teddy was halfway across the street when the courthouse door opened and a Marine in a dark green uniform came to the concrete landing and began shoveling snow. He waited until Teddy was about to ascend the first step before pausing in his shoveling. "You looking to enlist?"

Teddy stayed where he was next to the bottom step. "Yes Sir, I'm going to join the Navy."

The Marine laughed. "That's too bad."

"Why is that?"

"Well, in the Navy you're gonna be floating around on some rust bucket puking your guts out from being seasick. It'll probably hit a Montana cowboy like you pretty hard. You should consider the Marines."

Teddy came back, "I've heard the Marines spend a lot of time on boats too."

A surprised look came to the Marine's face. "Sometimes they do but there's an end point to it."

Teddy put his foot on the bottom step and said in a dismissive tone, "Sir, I've pretty much got my heart set on the Navy. I think it'd suit me."

"Well, I hope you didn't skip school to come over here to talk to those boys."

Thinking that he'd never be talking to this guy again, Teddy said, "What makes you think I'm in school."

The Marine broke out in a belly laugh that had Teddy turning red before he finally stopped. "You've got a dandy crop of peach fuzz. Three or four years from now it might even make a beard."

Teddy frowned and started up the steps. He was reaching for the door when the Marine said, "Don't embarrass yourself, son. They got a new man. He's by the book."

Teddy withdrew his hand from the door. He could feel the Marine's blue eyes upon him. He said, "My mother said she'd sign for me."

"How old are you?"

Another lie tumbled out. "Seventeen, Sir."

A wry smile came over the Marine's face. "You got a birth certificate to back that up?"

Teddy's hesitation gave away the prospect of another lie.

"No more bullshit, kid. I'm trying to do you a favor."

"You don't know my circumstances."

He smirked. "Let me guess. Broken home. Struggling to make it." He paused and laughed briefly before saying in a softer tone. "I been there, kid. This is more about escaping than wanting to do your patriotic duty and go kill japs. Am I right?"

Teddy could smell the Marine's aftershave. His demeanor oozed a confidence that Teddy couldn't see himself ever having. He nodded. "You're pretty much right."

"So, how old are you?"

"May 17th I'll be 16."

The Marine put his hand on Teddy's shoulder. "You should go home. Don't be so anxious to die."

Teddy seemed oblivious to the advice. "I know other guys who have lied about their age and got in."

"They slipped through the cracks."

"One of 'em told me the recruiter looked the other way."

"He might just look himself to the South Pacific too."

"You don't want to go?"

The man snorted. "You've seen too many movies, kid."

Teddy noted the Marine's graying hair around his temples and the multiple stripes on his sleeve. Instantly he felt ashamed. "I'm sorry, I didn't mean-"

The Marine cut him off. "I've done my time in combat. There's no glory in it. You should go home. Be a kid. Hope the war's over by the time you're old enough and they come looking for you."

For a moment, Teddy stood there uncertain what to do. Go inside. Go home. Finally, he said, "And if I come back, will you help me?"

The Marine stared hard at Teddy for a few seconds and then sighed heavily. "You don't know what you're asking for." And then he went back to shoveling snow.

CHAPTER TEN

There was little privacy in the cook shack. Last night Teddy had been hard-pressed to find a time when he could study his mother's handwriting in a letter that she had written several weeks ago to her mother in Kansas but had never mailed. Teddy had seen it all wadded up among spud peelings and empty tin cans in the five gallon bucket to the right of the sink that served as their garbage can. He normally wouldn't pick through the trash for anything, even something important, on account of Tom, who chewed plug tobacco, spit in it. However, in that house the possibility of anybody but him writing something on paper was extremely rare. He had waited until his mother went to the bathroom before retrieving the letter and stuffing it in his pocket. Alone in his room, he unwrinkled the single page.

January 14, 1942
Dear Mother,

> *I hope all is well with you. Is your arthritis bothering you this winter? I sure hope not. We are still on the Whitworth ranch out north of Elkhorn, Montana. There is much snow here and it is miserably cold. Tom has steady work here but grouses as to the nature of it most days. There are times it makes for much unpleasantness. I used to think it was the*

weather that made him this way, but I have come to the belief that is just how he is. Some days I think that I can't tolerate another like it. I hate to bring my troubles to you as I know you've got your own, but I and Teddy would like to come on the train for a visit this winter, maybe for good. I am ashamed to say, however, that I am without funds as Tom keeps a tight hold on his wallet and I work only here in the house. To that end, I was hoping that you could loan me enough money to make the trip. In time, I could repay you. I am confident that I could find work there and I have an old car that needs repairs but I'm certain it's worth something to the right person. Please think about it,

Your Loving Daughter,
Agnes

The contents of the letter had not come as any real surprise to Teddy. He knew that his mother wasn't happy. No one in that house was happy. Not his mother or Tom or him. Agnes should have mailed the letter, not that it would have done much good but at least she could say she tried. That's what Teddy was doing, trying to escape before he was permanently sucked into an even worse situation. To that end, he had tried his best to duplicate his mother's handwriting in the note that he was writing to use at school the next day.

Teddy walked right into the front office as carefree as you please and handed the note to Mrs. Watkins, a fortyish plump woman with brown hair and cat eye glasses. Before she even looked at it, she said, "You're first period class reported you absent."

"Sorry, I had a doctor's appointment."

"Umm," she said as she read the note.

Teddy had written a half dozen versions of the note before calling it good. It read:

>*Please excuse Teddy from 1ˢᵗ period history today. He has a doctor's appointment at 8:15.*
>
>*Thank You,*
>*Mrs. Agnes Kinney*

"Which doctor did you go to?"

There was something about the tone of Mrs. Watkins' voice that suggested to Teddy he was being baited into a trap. On the surface it seemed like an innocent question. In his mind he'd decided of the two doctors in town that he would pick Dr. Egbert since his office was closest to the school. His fate would have been sealed in the next few seconds if it hadn't been for Becky Sowards, a cute Mormon girl typing at the desk behind Mrs. Watkins. She was mouthing the name, *BREWER*. Teddy came close to tripping over his tongue but corrected his lie. "I went to Doc Brewer clear on the other side of town. That's why I'm so late."

Becky smiled while Mrs. Watkins frowned and looked the note over again. She was about to send Teddy off to class when the door to her right opened and out stepped the principal. He said, his voice as serious as a past due bill, "Mr. Walker, I've been waiting for you."

Teddy's voice registered both fear and surprise. "You have?"

The principal, a man with totally white hair and a clean shaven pockmarked face, smiled in a devious way. "A little bird told me they saw you at the courthouse this morning."

"They must have been mistaken."

"I don't think so."

"I'm sorry, Mr. Sperry, but it wasn't me."

Sperry took a step closer to Teddy and softened his demeanor slightly. "I appreciate your zeal to serve our country but you're still a boy. You need to stay right where you're at."

"I don't know that school is for me."

Sperry shook his head. "Trust me son, it is. Now, go on to class. But if there is anymore of this, I'll be contacting the truant officer."

Teddy came back with a hint of defiance in his voice. "Come spring, I'll be sixteen and I won't have to come here anymore."

The principal smiled derisively. "You do that, Teddy. The country can always use more ditch diggers." And then he turned, as if Teddy no longer existed, and went back into his office. Mrs. Watkins, who remained silent, followed suit going back to her desk next to the wall beneath a picture of President Roosevelt. An awkward air had descended on the room. Only Becky, who he'd been told had a crush on him, looked his way. She smiled. It was polite and weak, more like she pitied him. Teddy gave a brief chest high wave, almost like he was a school crossing guard. Her expression did not change. He walked on. They'd gotten the better of him, the school, the recruiters, his mother, life. At least today they had.

CHAPTER ELEVEN

The mystery of geometry was compounded in Teddy's mind by the defeats he had suffered that morning. They played heavily denying him any fantasy of exchanging his new life at the cook shack for one of adventure in the Navy. Nonetheless, he had worked up an appetite. Because the Elkhorn School District was semi destitute, they could offer only one hot lunch program and that was at the elementary school across town. The reason for it being there was that it would be safer for the older kids to leave the school grounds and travel that far as opposed to the little kids having to go elsewhere. And too, many of the older kids would not lower themselves to eat cafeteria food and would go downtown to eat. That is, those kids whose parents could afford it would. Teddy, however, was not among this group. In fact, the whole lunch thing was just another source of humiliation for him. Students had to present a lunch ticket, a piece of heavy yellow paper with your name on it and five black boxes beneath it. One ticket was good for a week or until all of the boxes had a punch hole. Meals were a quarter a piece unless you submitted a form showing how much money your parents made. If their income was below a certain level their kid ate for free. The tickets all looked the same but the people who sold them at the front office could never keep a secret. It was, therefore, mostly common knowledge that Teddy ate for free.

Classes let out promptly at noon. The lunch bus, which parked midway between the high school and the junior high left at 12:05 sharp. Betty, a heavyset woman with dark hair, who drove the bus was a stickler about being on time. Teddy had learned this the hard way during the fall semester when he'd gotten there just as the bus was driving off. He was certain that she saw him in her outside mirror as he chased after the bus. Her response was to shift into third gear and pull away. Today, however, was different, he had two minutes to spare.

"Where's your friend?"

Teddy turned around to see Becky coming towards him. He felt his chest get fluttery. "You mean, Jimmy?"

Becky laughed. "Yes, I thought you two always went to lunch together."

He instantly thought, *she must take note of what I do.* The fluttering got a little more intense. Aloud, he said, "He saw on the bulletin board that they was havin' tacos and refried beans today. Said he didn't care for it and was going down to the Owl."

"Must be nice to have that kind of money."

It instantly registered with Teddy that she'd said this for his benefit, like they were in the same financial boat. He knew better as he took note of her too. She dressed nice wearing lots of different clothes and she wasn't a regular on the lunch bus. She was a town kid. Her dad owned the grocery store. Teddy laughed in a friendly way, "I wouldn't know." He then stepped aside to let her on the bus first. He'd never thought they would sit together with her being cute, rich and a cheerleader to boot, but when they came to an empty seat in the third row she glanced back at him. "Wanna sit here?"

Teddy's heart went into high gear, hammering his chest cavity. His voice was shaky. "Sure."

Becky smiled and sat down next to the window. Teddy sat next to her. The effect she was having on him was reflected in his eyes. Out of the blue she said, "Why is it you hate school so much?"

Teddy hesitated. He'd not expected to have to bare his soul. He pondered telling her that it was his home life he hated the most and that to escape it by the route he was pursuing meant he'd have to quit school. But to open that can of worms might necessitate going into his life, living over the Lariat Bar or Owl Café or living with Tom and now life in the cook shack. No, he couldn't tell her that. She'd look upon him as pathetic white trash. He said, barely making eye contact, "It just ain't for me. Besides, there's a war going on."

"We're kids, Teddy."

Teddy frowned. "I've done man's work on the ranch plenty of times."

She said, trying not to be argumentative, "Don't you think it would be different in the service?"

"You don't think I can cut it?"

"That's not what I'm saying. I just think it might not be how you've got it pictured."

The giddy adrenaline that moments ago flooded Teddy's system was giving way to disappointment on its way to anger. "I ain't stupid, Becky. I know guys in the service not much older than me. If they can do it, I can too."

Becky paused. A look of uncertainty came over her as she appeared to study Teddy's face. The silence between them was getting awkward when she said, "Maybe you should pray about what's the right thing to do."

It was hard for Teddy to admit as it fit right in with his own self-image of not being as good as most people. He said, barely above a whisper, "I ain't never been to church."

"Not ever?"

"No."

"That's hard to believe."

"So, do you think less of me?"

"No, it's just all my friends go to church."

Becky's face started to turn red even before Teddy spoke, but he did not temper his words. "So, I guess I can't be your friend?"

She laughed briefly in a nervous way. "Sure, you can."

Teddy could see it in her face, hear it in her voice. There was no disguising it. She would never be his girlfriend in the sense he wanted. It would be nothing but a polite smile and a *hi* in the hall. Gone was any fantasy of writing her if he ever did join the Navy. At that moment his life seemed like a dream that had teased him for a time like it might turn out good. Today, he woke up to reality.

They did not sit together at lunch. A couple of girls who apparently qualified as friends called out to Becky. She said to Teddy, "See you later."

Teddy did his best to act like she hadn't hurt his feelings, he replied, "Ok."

Becky, however, did not hear him as she was giggling, walking away with her friends, already in another world. Either she was oblivious to what she'd just done, or she didn't care. It may have been that, from afar, Teddy was a fantasy of hers. That he would fit in her world. And now, after barely scratching the surface of who he was, she was done with him. In his mind's eye, Teddy laughed at himself. He'd seen the nice house in town where Becky lived. The image of her coming to the cook shack caused a sardonic grin to come to his face. *That'd go over 'bout like a turd in a punch bowl.* He sighed pulling the grin back while setting his food tray down on a near empty table as far away from Becky as he could get. He began picking at his meal wearing his embarrassment and anger like an outrageous Halloween costume, certain that everyone could see that he had been snubbed and was sitting alone. *She's a flirt, a silly girl flirt. Damn her. Why didn't she just leave me alone.* He'd mostly eaten one of his two tacos, but not much else, when he stood up and started towards the garbage can by the door to scrape his tray. He was mid scrape when a familiar voice sounded. "You know our troops could use that."

Teddy looked up. It was Mr. Pearson, a gruff, stocky teacher who was the lunchroom monitor and ticket puncher. He would know, better than anyone, that Teddy ate for free. Normally, Teddy ate everything he was given as he'd known hunger and being at the mercy of someone else for food. Today was different. He just wanted to be out of the lunchroom so people wouldn't be wondering, as he was certain they were, why he was sitting by himself. He said, "Sorry, I'm not feeling good."

"Well, maybe you shouldn't have taken so much."

In his defense, Teddy wanted to tell Pearson that he had slid his tray along and the kitchen ladies just dished it up the same for everybody, but he figured that would be perceived as arguing, so he said again, "Sorry."

Pearson did not lower his voice. "Don't abuse what the taxpayers are giving you."

Teddy snapped. He looked at the teacher in a hateful, insubordinate way. "This is the first time in a long time that I haven't cleaned up my plate and you're on my ass. It ain't right."

"You better watch your mouth, son. You're getting real close to being in a peck of trouble."

The real Teddy had lost control. The voice that came from his mouth shouted, "Screw you and the pig you rode in here on."

Angry shock registered on Pearson's face. Knowing, but not caring, that everyone in the lunchroom was looking at him and Teddy, he fired back, "You can expect to be called into the principal's office this afternoon. That smart mouth of yours has just earned you a vacation from school."

The lunchroom clamor had died away. Even among the little kids. Only one of the kitchen ladies was unaware. She was a big woman in a knee length white dress. Her dark hair was all bound up under a hair net. Glen Miller's, *In The Mood*, was playing on the radio. She was bobbing side to side as she washed a big stainless steel pot in the deep sink with steaming hot water. By and by she became aware of the obvious quiet in the lunchroom and the other two ladies standing dead still staring out through the opening above the counter. She immediately stopped, while Glen Miller did not, and aligned her focus with the other spectators. For the finale, Teddy left his bravado unchecked, he shouted, "Fine, you'd be doing me a favor." He then made his exit to the echo of Glen Miller playing in the kitchen.

Dusk had a firm grip on the Phillips ranch headquarters when Teddy got off the school bus and started down the road towards the cook shack. It was cold, such that the snow squeaked under foot and his eyes were watery and his nose was running. Before today he might have countered the cold with imagining himself in the warmth of Navy boot camp in San Diego. Now, that seemed to be some cruel joke that he'd played on himself.

As he expected, the lights were on in the cook shack and blue smoke was pouring straight up from the stovepipe. Supper time was thirty minutes away. He opened the door to warmth and good smells. He savored these senses just briefly until his mother noticed he had an armful of textbooks. She stared at them in an obvious way before looking him in the eyes. "You get a big homework assignment."

"I got kicked out."

Agnes shrieked. "Kicked out?"

"Yeah, I sassed a teacher."

"Why?"

"He got on me for not cleaning my plate up at lunch."

Anger danced in her eyes. "You know better than that, especially with the government rationing."

Teddy thought to tell her all that was going on in his head, but he knew she could no more fix it than him. He shrugged. "It's been a long day, Ma."

"So, how long you out for?"

Teddy hesitated. He knew the first part of his punishment would make her mad, but the second part would flat piss her off. He eased the words out like they were in a heavy bucket that had to be let down gently. "I can't go back to school for a week." He paused and then added, "At the lunchroom, I'm banned for the rest of the year."

"What?"

"Sorry, Ma."

Agnes sighed heavily as she gave Teddy a dirty look. She shook her head. "You're costing me money I ain't got. You're gonna have to pack a lunch and I ain't got time to make it and cook for all these men. So, guess what?"

Teddy wanted to say that he would just quit school but then he recalled the principal saying he would put the truancy officer on him if he was late again. "I know, Ma. I can do that."

Agnes scoffed. "Well, can you come up with the money to pay for what goes in those lunches?"

"Sorry, Ma."

Agnes frowned and reached for a smoldering cigarette in an ashtray sitting on the counter. She took a long draw on it and blew the smoke out towards Teddy. "I need for you to set the table. Put an extra plate on. George hired some stew bum he got out of one of the bars in town."

At supper that night Pete was his usual self, all full of blow and go dominating the conversation. Teddy was cutting a bite of pork chop while replaying the lunchroom events when Pete abruptly went away from docking lambs and invaded his thoughts. He boomed from the far end of the table. "So, Mr. Teddy, how goes your quest to sail the seven seas?"

Teddy looked at Pete. He felt like he was making fun of him and didn't deserve an answer. Still, he'd learned the hard way today that it wasn't smart being disrespectful to adults regardless of what they'd said. He came back, almost sullen. "Not good."

"Well, did ya talk to the swabbies?"

"No, I ran into this old Marine guy. He said it wouldn't do no good."

"Now, there's the outfit you wanna join."

"He told me to go home."

Pete slurped up some hot coffee. "That was probably good advice. A young fella like you shouldn't be lookin' for ways to die."

Teddy said, purposely hoping to draw Pete out about his time in the Marines. "You did."

Surprise came to Pete's face followed by him looking at Agnes whom he suspected had told Teddy about his time in France. Her expression was slightly mystified. "That was different. I didn't have a choice."

Teddy was saved from having to respond to Pete by the old stew bum, Charlie Graves, picking up a full glass of milk with both hands and trembling it to his mouth. He was an example of what a three day whiskey drunk can do to an old man. As he lowered the glass a rivulet of milk ran from the corner of his mouth down his chin. He seemed unaware that it was there. And then he said, his bloodshot watery eyes focused on Teddy, "I got gassed over there. You should listen to these people."

Teddy nodded, hoping to end the conversation. "Yeah, I reckon so."

CHAPTER TWELVE

By late February Teddy and his mother had settled into the cook shack as best they could. George had told Agnes it was ok to add a woman's touch to it. To back that up, on a trip to town he had allowed her to pick out some brown cloth and curtain rods for the two windows in her room and the other three out in the kitchen. He even allowed her to come to his house and sew the curtains on his dead wife's sewing machine. And so began the gossip.

It was Saturday morning, not long after breakfast. Teddy was feeding and watering the ewes and newborn lambs in one of the canvas covered sheds. A row of small individual pens, just big enough for a ewe and her lamb, lined each of the long sides of the shed. That being about 150 feet. An alleyway about five feet wide was left between the rows to allow for dragging a water hose, bales of hay or moving the sheep in and out of the pens. A small space just big enough for a coal burning stove was left near the door on each end of the shed. On a cold day like today was, with it spitting snow outside, Teddy's job was good duty. He had started with feeding. There were V-shaped slotted hay racks for each pen that had to be filled every morning from the pile of bales stacked just outside the shed. He had carried several bales inside, cut the wires on one of them and was breaking off flakes about four inches thick and stuffing them into the hay racks. To Teddy it was easy work but, nonetheless, man's work. It caused his mind to drift back to that day on the lunch bus and his conversation with Becky. That's where he was at when he heard snippets of voices mixed in with the roar of the tractor and hay wagon pull up outside and shut down. Pete and Frank continued their conversation as they began to unload the hay.

"So, you figure ole George is beddin' her down?"

Pete laughed in a sinister way. "You think all she did was sew curtains while she was in his house?" He paused and laughed again. "If that's the case, you better think again."

Frank came back. "Well, I guess her being your ex sister in-law you would know better than me."

"Yeah, she's no goody two shoes. I can tell ya that."

Frank gave an expectant laugh. "She like to earn a few bucks off her backside, does she?"

For a moment, Teddy could hear nothing but the stabs of the hay hooks going into the bales and the grunts of the men as they stacked them. Pete came back with a laugh, always a laugh. "Let's just say she's easily persuaded."

Like a skilled interrogator Frank added, "You sound like you got firsthand knowledge on this matter."

Again, there was silence before Pete replied but this time there was no laugh. "I ain't proud of it, her being my brother's wife."

"Well, your brother's dead ain't he?"

"He wasn't at the time."

"Oh."

"It was just one of those things."

Moments later the tractor started and rumbled away in the direction of the half sheds. Pete and Frank, ignorant of the hurt they'd caused Teddy, were now bantering about the arrival of spring. Teddy, on the other hand, teared up just short of crying, kept on stuffing hay in the racks as the naysayer within him passed judgement. *Damn her. Is there no end to this crap?*

On Sunday, Teddy worked only till noon on account of he had two tests at school the next day. One in geometry and the other in history. Agnes had asked George if it would be ok for Teddy to take the afternoon off to study. He'd readily agreed to it while a month ago, pre curtains, he'd said that Teddy working during his suspension from school would be a good way to pay for his lunches. At the time, his tone suggested either Teddy worked, or the cost of his lunches would be deducted from his mother's pay. Things were different now.

Since that day in the covered shed when he'd overheard Pete and Frank, Teddy's opinion, his image of how he saw his mother had slipped a couple of notches. He did not like to think of her as a slut. In the past he'd rationalized her liaisons with men as necessary to their survival and her being a widow. But now, she was married. Tom, as bad as he was, was still her husband until death or the court caused them to part. Her and Pete, though, that was grounds for God to send them both to hell. The morality of all this worked on Teddy like a leaning tree in the wind. It prodded him over and over until he looked up from his geometry book to his mother at the sink doing the dishes from lunch. "Ma, tell me again how it was that Pa was killed."

Agnes paused but didn't turn around. "Why do you ask?"

"I don't know. Just popped into my mind."

Agnes sighed. "I don't like to think about it, Teddy. It was a damned fool thing for your father to do turning those horses loose."

"The fight was at a dance, right."

Agnes frowned. "You know what happened. Why are you making me tell you again?"

"I don't know. I was so little I just don't remember anything about it."

"Well, you were barely a year old."

How long were you guys married before he died?"

"Almost five years."

"That's a long time."

"Yes, it is."

"Do you ever wish you'd had more kids than just me?"

A peculiar, knowing look came to Agnes' face but she did not pursue it, saying only, "You better do your studies."

CHAPTER THIRTEEN

Loneliness is a powerful thing. It was the third week of March and there was little evidence that spring would be happening anytime soon, at least on Icehouse Creek there wasn't. The weather Gods would occasionally allow a teaser day of sunshine and then follow it up with a big dump of snow. Everybody was sick of winter. So, it came as no surprise to Teddy that on the last Sunday afternoon of the month, when he was bringing an armful of wood in from the woodshed, he saw Tom's pickup coming up the road. He cursed before looking away and going inside the cook shack. Shortly, he heard the truck's motor shut off and one door slam. Teddy's heart raced as his mind went back to the night Tom punched him. He briefly considered arming himself with a stick of firewood but then thought better of it as that would likely antagonize him. He stood there staring at the door, waiting for the knock. And then it came, prodding his heart to go even faster. He did not move. *If I don't open the door, he'll get the message and leave.* A second knock came. "Teddy, I saw you go in there."

Fear, tempered with hate, kept Teddy from moving. He'd locked the door but knew as big as Tom was, he could easily kick it in.

"C'mon. Teddy, open up."

Teddy looked at the door's latch and envisioned the consequences of pissing Tom off to the point he broke the door down. He shouted, "Whaddaya want?"

Teddy heard Tom's exaggerated sigh of anger and frustration followed by, "I want you and your mother to come home. I miss you guys."

Teddy scoffed and said to himself, *He don't miss me at all. What he misses is sleepin' with ma and having her cook for him and wash his clothes.* He wanted to give Tom his best sarcastic laugh, but he checked his tongue saying instead, "We like it here, Tom."

The old Tom surfaced, he laughed, "In this dump?"

Teddy couldn't help himself. "I ain't been beat up not once since we been here."

"No need to get smart about it, Teddy. That was a bad night. You just set me off."

Teddy told himself, *Ain't gonna argue with him. He'll blow up sure as hell.* It got quiet for a time and then in the window to the right of the door was Tom's face up close to the glass looking in between the new curtain halves. Tom said, like he already knew part of the answer, "Where's your ma gone to?"

"I don't know."

"Teddy, my patience for your bullshit is about to run out. Now where's your mother? I wanna talk to her."

Teddy knew exactly where his mother was. Agnes had given him specific instructions. Keep a fire under the big kettle of beef stew slow cooking on the stove and a pan of apple cobbler in the oven. The cobbler was due to come out in about ten minutes. After that, two dozen sourdough rolls that would have finished raising by then were to go in the oven. She would be back in time to put supper on the table, she'd said. Teddy thought about lying. Telling Tom that she'd gone to town. To which he'd likely come back with, *on a Sunday afternoon? What for? Who'd she go with?* And he'd be obliged to prop the first lie up with several more and then Tom would tire of it all and jerk Teddy up by his collar and threaten to slap the dog shit out of him if he didn't come clean right then and there. In a moment of indifference, the naysayer within Teddy shouted out, *she did this to herself*. His conscience having granted him permission to rat his mother out, Teddy told the truth, "She's up to George's listening to a radio program."

The look on Tom's face was instant hurt that suddenly morphed into anger when he saw the new radio sitting on a straight back wooden chair next to the couch. George had bought the radio to keep Teddy company since his mother seldom slept in the cook shack anymore. Tom jabbed his index finger in the direction of the radio. "What's wrong with that one?"

Teddy thought about lying, *it don't work*. The truth, or close to it, was already loaded on his tongue. "I guess she just wanted some grownup company."

Tom sneered. "If you weren't a snot-nosed kid I'd tell you what kind of company she wants."

Teddy stared back at Tom like he was as naïve as Tom thought he was. For a moment they were locked on to one another before Tom stomped away and roared off in his pickup towards George's house.

Within seconds, Tom was through the perimeter of tall pines that mostly hid George's place. He parked next to George's pickup mumbling as he got out, "Listening to a radio my ass." The snow had melted off the south facing green shingles of the big log structure but not the lawn all around it. Belly deep to a dog, it was peppered with tracks and yellow holes. Hog wire stretched between wood posts surrounded it all. A gate made of weathered vertical boards defined the beginning of a flat rock path to the front door. Tom flung the gate open with far more force than necessary and left it. A large picture window was to the side of the entrance.

Through it he could see a radio encased in honey oak sitting on a table between two black padded chairs. Above it was the mount of a bighorn sheep. To the right of that was a huge rock fireplace. Yellow flames caressed a jumbled pile of wood within it. Tom scoffed saying to himself, *She's in the money now*. He paused just short of the door and continued his visual search of the living room. It was grand, yet cozy and inviting. A far cry from the cookshack. It was what owning 5,000 head of sheep could buy you. But they were not there. Carnal images of them flooded his mind. His anger pulsed even harder. He was tempted to not knock. Just walk right in on them. He would be justified. Another man having his way with another's wife. He allowed the probable consequences of him catching them in bed to briefly play in his mind. George, close to fifty, twenty pounds lighter. Tom was confident he'd whip his ass. And Agnes, she'd get hers' too. Tom turned the doorknob and stepped inside quietly closing the door behind him. He could hear the radio now, just barely. The music was not lively. It seemed to compliment the rhythmic ticking of the grandfather clock across the room. To his left the smell of coffee floated out from the kitchen. His heart was hammering. Beyond the padded chairs was a hallway. From his vantage point one door was visible. Half open, it appeared to be a bathroom. *Got to be where the bedrooms are*, he said to himself. The first step in his rubber overshoes upon the dark hardwood floor went well. Quiet as a mouse. The second, not so good. Dull, muffled voices sounded down the hall. Tom took another step. Once again, the floorboards, put down by George's father, betrayed Tom. The voices now became excited. Their paranoia of being discovered about to be validated. Tom was torn if he should go on. He no longer had the element of surprise. Suddenly, it became moot as George emerged from the hall wearing just his Levi's. He shouted, "What the hell are you doing in my house, Kinney?"

Tom scoffed defiantly. "Like you don't know you bed robbing sonovabitch."

George started towards Tom, his demeanor angry and threatening. He stopped within a few feet of him and laughed sarcastically. "You fool, you had nothing to steal."

"She's my wife."

"On paper maybe."

And then, as if the fire between the two men could burn no hotter, Agnes, fully dressed except for her boots, stepped from the hallway to the side of George.

Tom became enraged. "Agnes, get your ass over here. You're going home."

Agnes laughed in his face. "Home, with you? That's not home, Tom. That's hell."

Tom started toward her. "I ain't got the money mister big shot here does but you're still my wife."

"You threw me and Teddy out. Did you forget that?"

George blocked Tom's path to Agnes. The salt and pepper hair on his chest rising and falling with his angry, excited breathing. "You need to leave. Get off my ranch."

Tom looked at George, said nothing and then sucker punched him with a massive right hand. Stunned, George staggered backwards. Before he could regain his wits, Tom was pummeling his face and body. Blood was already spewing from his nose and lips. Agnes screamed as she grabbed at Tom's arms. "Stop it, Tom. Stop it. You sonovabitch, stop it. He's hurt. That's enough." Tom barely paused as he backhanded Agnes hard knocking her against the wall. George, who'd gone to the floor, was trying to get up when Tom began kicking him with his heavy overshoe covered cowboy boots. "Steal my wife, will ya, you old bastard." His anger was insatiable. And then the pandemonium, the violence, went a notch higher as the 30-30 roared. The 170 grain soft nose bullet entered Tom's back a little ways below his left shoulder blade. Its trajectory being such that it plowed right into his raging heart and pretty much pureed it. Still, it took a few seconds for it to register with him that he was dead. He turned in kind of a wobbly stagger to see what had hit him in the back. His expression of surprise, or intense shock, did not change when he came face to face with the rifle that Agnes was holding. When he toppled over, it was in her direction.

A 30-30 makes a fair amount of noise outdoors. But if it's fired inside a house some distance away a person hearing it might not pay it much heed. Teddy, on the other hand, having told Tom where his mother was at, heard the dull whomp and assumed the worst. He had just stepped outside when he saw Pete's pickup on his way to the little blue and white camp trailer where he lived to the east of the cook shack. He gave a high, frantic wave causing Pete to steer his way. From the cab of his truck, Pete said, "What's going on?"

"I think I heard a gunshot over at George's."

"Well, you know he's got that chicken coop behind his house. Maybe he was shootin' at a fox or coyote."

"My mom's up there and so's Tom."

"Holy shit."

Teddy started for the passenger side of Pete's truck.

Pete shouted. "You better stay here."

"C'mon, Pete."

He slipped the truck in gear. "No, in fact you go over to Frank's sheep camp. Wait for me there. He's got a gun."

Pete backed around, changed gears and stabbed the accelerator. The rear end of his pickup sashayed sending rooster tails of snow in the air. And then he eased off the gas, got traction and within seconds he disappeared through the trees around George's house. Even before he came to a stop, he was groping beneath the seat for his holstered .45 automatic. Being a convicted felon, he was not supposed to possess any kind of firearm but if he'd been one to obey the law, he would never have been a felon in the first place.

Pete parked behind Tom's pickup and bailed out in a semi crouch. He looked over the hood of his pickup at the same picture window that Tom had. At first, he could see nothing but the bighorn sheep on the wall and the big rock chimney. In his mind the most likely scenario played out that the single gunshot was Tom killing George and now he was doing whatever to Agnes. The thought of it caused him to chamber a round in his pistol and start towards the still open gate. He'd just passed through it when he saw movement in the house. It was Agnes. Seconds later she burst out the front door, but stopped right there. She was sobbing. Her face and hands were bloody. Tears, copious tears, were streaming down her cheeks cutting trails through the blood. She cried, "Pete, Pete, I need your help."

He gauged her fear to be near hysterical and quickened his pace. Before he could reach her, she wailed loudly, "Oh, Pete, I've done a terrible thing." And then she went back inside leaving the door wide open. He followed her, his mind awash in images of what might await him. Mired in this unpleasantness was the near indifference she treated him with at the cook shack. Now, it was Pete, *I need your help*. Suddenly, she stopped. Pete came along side of her. Lying face down in a pool of blood was Tom. Right in front of the radio and padded chairs.

Agnes put her hands to her face and began to sob. Her upper torso rocked in sync with her grief. "I shot him, Pete. I killed him."

George said, from the couch over by the fireplace, "She didn't have a choice. The sonovabitch was puttin' the boot to me."

Agnes sobbed again. "I didn't, Pete. It was awful. He's a cruel man."

It might be a stretch to say that Pete and Tom were friends, but they knew one another. They had gotten drunk together at the Lariat a couple of weeks ago. At breakfast the next morning he'd told the guys how they'd, *played pool and chased the dollies till almost milkin' time*. It had occurred to him that maybe he should leave out the dollies part for Agnes' benefit, but he did not and absorbed her scowl in the telling. Now here he was standing over the body of his drinking buddy and next to the woman who despised him because of their infidelity. It seemed to Pete that she and her latest lover, or meal ticket, or whatever label fit George, were rehearsing for what they would tell the Sheriff. Pete suddenly became aware that the hammer was back on his pistol. He pointed the gun down and to the side as he lowered the hammer.

George called out, his voice un-steady, full of pain, "See, even you came ready to shoot. What would you have done if you'd walked in the midst of all this?"

"I would've asked Tom to stop."

George snorted and grimaced with pain. "Easy for you to say. You're weren't the one getting' the shit kicked out of you."

Pete thought to say, *I wasn't the one screwing his wife*, but then the fact that George controlled his economic well-being took hold of his tongue. "Yeah, George, you do have a point." And then looking at George's bloodied chest and face and hands, he added, "How bad are you hurt?"

George scrunched his face up in pain. "I believe I need to go to the hospital. Hurts to breathe and I can't get my nose to stop bleeding."

Agnes said, "Can you drive us to town?"

Pete nodded. "Sure, at some point though we gotta call the sheriff."

George came back sharp and abrupt. "We'll call him from the damned hospital."

CHAPTER FOURTEEN

Because it hurt too much to sit up on the pickup seat, they put George in a sleeping bag so he could lay in the back. Agnes bundled herself in a heavy coat and stocking hat and quilt and sat next to him like they were in love. It did speak well of her, or so she thought, that she insisted they stop and get Teddy. He, and Frank, still cradling his Winchester 25-35, were standing in front of the cook shack when Pete pulled up in George's truck, a better vehicle for the trip to town. From the back of the pickup Agnes called out, her face a mere porthole in the shroud of the quilt. "Teddy, come get in."

Teddy looked over at Frank. He said, barely above a whisper, "She should never have been up there."

Frank sighed and shook his head. "No, it generally ain't good to fish in the company pond."

Agnes yelled again. "Hurry, Teddy."

When he was close enough to the truck that he could see George laid out, a peculiar thing happened. It wasn't that he cared, but for some reason he asked the obvious, "Where's Tom?"

"Just get in, Teddy."

Teddy got in the front with Pete not suspecting that he would be window dressing when the sheriff came to the hospital to question this poor mother who had shot her abusive husband in the back.

Pete put the truck in second gear and started off at a good clip, the day being even more somber now than the layers of gray whipped cream overhead had already made it. He said, knowing that it was coming, "Tom's dead."

A twinge of undefined adrenaline went through Teddy. He wasn't sad or happy. It was just that dying was a serious thing. There were no second chances for Tom now. He'd often thought Tom was destined to go to hell. He tried to envision what hell was like and if Tom was there. He said as Pete shifted to third, "So, what happened?"

"Your mother shot him."

"I always figured that someday it was gonna come to that."

"Well, today was that day."

It became quiet between them save for the growl of the pickup's engine struggling against the snow. Close to a mile of silence had gone by when Teddy asked, "Do you think Tom had it coming?"

Pete's mind instantly flashed back two weeks ago to him and Tom's drunken carousing in town. There had been dollies, but neither of them wanted to tie up for more than a night with a middle-aged hired hand that was going nowhere good in life. He wondered if this rejection and the foot of snow still on the ground with it being *damned near April* had caused Tom to see Agnes in a better light. "I don't know."

"You've got some doubts."

Before he considered the hypocrisy of it, Pete frowned and said, "Well, legally your ma and Tom are still married."

"So, you think George got what he deserved?"

"Hell, I don't know, Teddy. It was your ma that poked this hornet's nest. Everybody might have been better off if she would've just tended to her biscuits."

In his mind's eye Teddy went back to that day in the sheep shed and eavesdropping on Pete and Frank. It had planted a suspicion within him that likely only his mother or Pete could clear up. He was tired of wondering or waiting for the right time or just trying to put it out of mind. He spit it out. "Was that how it was with you and her?"

"What?"

"She should have tended to her biscuits."

"You know?"

Teddy nodded.

Pete sighed and then looked back at the road like it needed his full attention. After a half mile or so, he manned up, "It wasn't all her doing."

"So, it's true?"

"I ain't proud of it. We'd been drinkin'. Your pa wasn't home, and things just got out of hand."

Teddy looked at Pete's face. He could see himself in his nose and chin. His mother had told him, *you've got that Walker nose*, like it was common to all of them. Teddy, on the other hand, never saw that nose, that slight hump, that parrot beak in anybody but Pete and him. Certainly, not his father. He came back. "Are you my father?"

Pete laughed nervously. "I don't think so."

"You know, I'm not just a dumb kid."

Pete reached in his pocket for his cigarettes. "Never said you were."

"Ma was married to my dad for five years and no kids. Then you come along."

Pete lit his cigarette and cracked his window to let the smoke out. Finally, he looked over at Teddy. "As far as I'm concerned, I'm your uncle." He then turned on the radio and cranked up the volume.

CHAPTER FIFTEEN

By the time they got into Elkhorn lights were on in the houses. Through some of the windows Teddy could see people, normal people, eating their supper. As they went by the Texaco a kid from school who worked there, recognized Teddy. He waved. Before he could stop himself, Teddy waved back. *Shit, he'll ask me tomorrow what I was doing in town and what do I say, oh my stepfather beat up my mother, so she killed him.*

Just past the grain elevator Pete turned right, bounced over the train tracks causing George to cry out cursing him for not knowing enough to slow down. Pete and Teddy, however, did not hear it over the radio. Pete drove on. First Street was bordered by more big cottonwoods and old houses with normal people. At the end of it, near the Elkhorn River, was the hospital, a one story, pale brown brick building. In the parking lot were three cars and a pickup with several bales of hay in its bed. A black dog with dirty matted hair was laying on the hay. Pete steered to the left of the vehicles and towards where the ambulance was parked beneath a canopy on the backside of the hospital. He parked behind the ambulance and had barely gotten out when he heard George groaning as he struggled to sit up. "Oh shit, Sweetie, I think I'm busted up pretty good inside."

Agnes said without looking at him, her tone curt almost like he was some dumb shit, "Pete, you wanna lend a hand here?"

Pete frowned briefly at her as he lowered the tailgate. Grabbing two fistfuls of the bottom edge of the sleeping bag he said, "George, I'm gonna drag you out to where you can lower your legs to the ground and then just stand up, alright?"

George nodded. "Let's give it a go."

The metal truck bed offered little resistance to George's 180 pounds. When his butt reached the hinged crevice between the bed and the hanging tailgate, Pete stopped and gently lowered the sleeping bag with his legs to the ground. He then stepped closer to George with his arms outstretched. "Gimme your hands."

George complied. "Be easy now."

Just like a draw bridge being raised, George stood up but not without complaint. "Damn, that hurts."

Agnes unzipped the sleeping bag and let it fall to the ground so that George could step out. She then allowed him to drape his right arm around her shoulder. They began hobbling towards the door with a sign above it that read: EMERGENCY ROOM. They were almost there when it opened and a husky, middle-aged woman with dark hair in powder blue scrubs came out. "Bring him on in." They all squeezed past the woman who was holding the door open. The room was bright, its lights reflecting somewhat off the green tile floor. She gestured to a skinny table with a flimsy paper covering in the center of the room. "Set him down here."

George leaned his butt against the end of the table.

She added. "Go ahead and lay down."

George wriggled, grunted and groaned further onto the table with Agnes' help and laid down.

The nurse glanced at Agnes and then back to George. "So, what happened. You guys in a car wreck?"

It was like somebody flipped a switch, the silence came over the room that quick. It was dead quiet save for the low hum of a white refrigerator in the corner of the room. Teddy looked on wondering what parts they were going to leave out. Agnes finally said, "We were in a fight."

The woman looked puzzled. "With one another?"

George stepped up. "No, her husband, Tom Kinney."

A grin escaped the nurse's face just long enough to make Agnes' turn a littler redder. She then became serious and picked up a clipboard with forms on it from the counter behind her. "I need to get some basic information before the doctor comes in. Where do you folks live?"

George offered. "Phillips Ranch, Rural Route 1, Elkhorn."

"Both of you?"

"Yes."

"Is that where this altercation took place?"

"Yes."

It was probably logical for the nurse to assume that since Agnes lived on the Phillips' ranch and that Tom Kinney was her husband that he did too. However, she may or may not have needed to know for sure, but she asked, "And Mr. Kinney lives at this same location?"

The white elephant returned to the room with friends. The nurse stood, her hand poised with pencil over the form. Finally, she looked up searching their faces, all of them pregnant with varying degrees of fear. The nurse, however, settled her eyes on Agnes. "Mr. Kinney, does he live on the ranch too?"

Agnes' bloodshot eyes instantly filled with tears that began to stream down either side of her broken nose. She looked pitiful, dried blood on her face and bits of toilet paper stuffed in her nostrils to stop the bleeding. After a time when everyone in the room was feeling sorry for her, she sobbed, "No, he's dead."

Shock flooded the nurse's face. "Dead?"

Agnes nodded, breathing heavily through her mouth to steady herself she said, "Yes, I killed him. I shot him. I had no choice."

A sudden fearful, uncomfortable look came into the nurse's eyes. It was like she just confirmed that the people in the room were wicked, that they were several caste levels beneath her. Her mind raced, fleeting glimpses of that morning's church service. *Adultery and now murder. What did she think was going to happen*? At last, she said without a hint of compassion, "Oh, I'll get the doctor now." And then she clutched the clipboard to her ample bosom, opened a door to the left of Teddy and Pete and was gone.

The door had barely closed behind the nurse when Teddy stepped to its small window and looked out. "She's talking to a fella that looks like he could be a doctor."

Pete looked over Teddy's shoulder. A middle-aged man with wire rim glasses and thinning hair wearing a white coat was looking intently at the nurse. Their expressions were serious. The doctor glanced at the door making eye contact with Pete and Teddy. It seemed to have repulsed him as, in the next instant, he and the nurse disappeared around the corner. Pete scoffed and whispered, mostly for his own benefit, "Going to call the law."

Teddy, his eyes big, looked around. Pete gently shook his head.

George called out in a pained voice. "What the hell is going on out there? A man could die in here while they're making up their mind what to do."

Pete looked at George and shrugged. "Dunno, George. You know how doctors are. Always keep ya waitin'."

"Well, I'm not in the mood for it tonight."

Agnes was standing beside the table holding George's left hand in both of hers. Pete said to himself, *if only she'd tended to her biscuits we wouldn't be here now*. He said aloud, "Believe I'll go have a smoke."

"Yeah, smoke one for me too," said George. And then he grimaced in pain.

Teddy followed Pete outside. It was full-on dark. A person would think that the hospital could have afforded a streetlight in the parking lot, but there was none. Pete spread the sleeping bag so that it would shield he and Teddy's backsides from the cold steel of the pickup bed. They sat with their legs hanging out the back. Pete lit a cigarette and blew the smoke out in a thoughtful way. "So, whaddaya think, Teddy?"

"About what?"

"All this."

"Kinda makes me wish I wasn't a Walker."

Pete snorted. "I've thought that a time or two myself."

"Yeah, but you're older. People can't boss you around like they can me."

Pete laughed. "You always got a boss, Teddy. I don't care who you are, except maybe God, everybody has to answer to somebody."

They went quiet while mulling the wisdom of what Pete had just said. And then Teddy, looking mostly at the glowing end of Pete's cigarette, came back, "I don't know that I can go back to school."

"You got to. You don't wanna end up like me."

Teddy hesitated, searching for words to disagree with. Finally, he said, "You're doing alright."

Pete laughed to the point it made him cough. By and by it subsided, allowing him to talk again. "Shit, Teddy, I got an eighth-grade education, a prison record, a beat-up pickup and less 'an twenty dollars to my name." He laughed sarcastically. "Yes sir, I'm doing alright."

"You were a Marine."

Pete snorted. "That and a nickel 'll get you a cup of coffee."

Before Teddy could respond, a rotating red light appeared in the darkness straight out from them in between the rows of houses where normal people lived eating their supper and listening to the radio. Pete said, "Well, here they come."

Teddy's voice was shaky. "Ma 'll be alright, won't she? It was self-defense."

Pete took a long draw of his cigarette and exhaled noisily. "I don't know. Tom had his fists. Your ma had a 30-30."

Teddy looked out at the red light alerting the normal people that there was gossip to be had. One of them, Teddy figured, would know somebody at the hospital they could call. Before bedtime the whole sordid mess at the Phillips ranch would be common knowledge to lots of folks. Teddy was certain of it. Moments later, the sheriff pulled his black pickup to a stop in front of where Pete and Teddy were sitting. They squinted and put up a hand to shield their eyes from his headlights and the incessant red orb. The sheriff, however, was indifferent to their discomfort and allowed the conspicuous lightshow to continue until he was done on the radio. Abruptly, it became dark and quiet, as he turned off his motor. He crunched through the snow stopping just short of Pete and Teddy. If not for the man's .38 Caliber Colt that rode high on his right hip, his green mackinaw and gray Stetson would have allowed him to pass for a rancher. He said in a confident tone, "You fellas part of that debacle out at the Phillips place?"

Pete, his arms folded across his chest with the first two fingers of his right hand holding his cigarette, said, "We brought the injured people in."

"And you are?"

"Pete Walker and this is my nephew, Teddy Walker."

The sheriff's head instantly bobbed. "Oh, so you're Pete Walker. Your parole officer was by to see me a couple weeks ago."

"Me too."

"Yeah, he said since he was all the way over in Billings that there might come a time when he'd ask me to fill in for him."

"Well, you know where I'm at."

Having established the fact that Pete's continued freedom could be dependent upon how the sheriff saw things, he said, "So, what I'm hearing is that Mrs. Kinney shot her husband?"

"Yeah, he was beatin' hell outta George and her."

"Was Mr. Kinney armed?"

"No."

"Well, how was it that Mrs. Kinney had a gun?"

Pete shrugged. "I don't know. I guess Tom was distracted beatin' on George and she slipped away. You need to ask her that."

The sheriff began in a good ole boy tone. "I will, in due time. You'd be amazed though how stories about the same thing can vary. It's like if you ask three different people, did it rain yesterday. One might say, oh hell yeah. It was a real frog strangler. And the second person might say, ah, it just sprinkled. And the third would say, dry as a bone yesterday. So, you see what I mean?"

Pete could see exactly what he meant. If he told him anything that was contradicted by George or Agnes, he could be charged with lying to a police officer or obstructing justice. Either one would be a violation of his parole and a ticket back to Deerlodge.

The sheriff allowed Pete time enough to consider his parable and take another draw on his cigarette. "So, how many times did Mrs. Kinney shoot her husband?"

Pete sensed where this was going. For Teddy's sake he wished that he could lie and get away with it. He fell in line like a calf going up the chute to be branded. He said, "Once."

"Where'd she shoot him at?"

"In the back."

Teddy gasped.

The sheriff echoed like he hadn't heard, "In the back?"

Pete's mind was spinning a lie. *She threw down on him with that 30-30 and asked him to stop kicking George and he laughed at her. Said she didn't have the balls to shoot him.* And then he recalled how her conscience just a few hours ago had held nothing back. George on the couch telling her it was alright. Pete continued on up the chute. "Yeah, in the back."

The sheriff shook his head. "I knew Tom Kinney. He was an onery cuss but not stupid. Do you know if once Mrs. Kinney had the gun, she warned Tom to stop before shooting?"

There it was. To lie or not. He could repeat Agnes' confession to him and George, but if they chose not to lie, he would be odd man out and on his way to Deerlodge. From the corner of his eye, he could see that Teddy was looking at him. Nonetheless, he said, "Mind you, she was upset but shortly after I got there, she said she just shot him."

"Without warning?"

"I believe so."

"What time was this?"

Teddy cut in. "4:35,"

The sheriff shifted his attention to Teddy. "You're sure on that time?"

"Yes, I was watching the clock. The cobbler was supposed to come out of the oven at a quarter till five and the rolls go in."

"So, your ma left you to do the cooking, huh?"

An uneasy silence followed with each of them expanding upon the implication of the sheriff's words. After his point had been made, he said, "I'm gonna go inside."

Pete waited until the emergency room door had closed. "I'm sorry, Teddy."

He shrugged. "I know you and Ma don't get along."

"That's your ma's doing, not mine. She thinks I'm just a worthless jailbird."

"It ain't got nothing to do with you and her, you know?"

Pete became quiet for a good while and then he said, "After that night her and I was together she got all addle brained. Wanted to leave your father so her and I could run off and get married."

"Why didn't you?"

Pete scoffed. "I couldn't do that to my brother."

Teddy snorted. "But you slept with his wife."

"And there's not a day goes by that I don't regret it." He paused. "Maybe that's why your ma despises me. I regret it and she doesn't."

Teddy stared out into the darkness down First Street with the houses where normal people lived and said, "Do you regret me?"

Pete took the last draw on his cigarette, exhaled and flipped the butt into the snow. He said, not looking at Teddy, "Too much water under the bridge now."

CHAPTER SIXTEEN

Pete purposely stayed outside, and Teddy with him, to allow things inside to unravel on their own. They'd been there long enough for Pete to smoke another cigarette when headlights appeared on First Street that did not turn in to any of the normal people's houses. By and by it was apparent that the lights were coming to the hospital. And then that creepy feeling that most people get when they see a hearse engulfed the two of them. The car was white, different than the snow, with white sidewall tires. It stopped behind the sheriff's pickup. Fred Snyder, owner of the town's only funeral home as well as being the county coroner, got out. He started towards them, his stride suggesting that he wasn't going to stop. In passing, he nodded, "Evening," and kept on going. Teddy felt slighted. It was dark but not that dark. He knew Fred Snyder. He was father to Herb Snyder, one of his friends. About two years ago, before his mother's car broke down, Teddy had gone to Herb's birthday party. He'd shook Fred's hand even though it made him uncomfortable knowing that it handled dead people on a regular basis. And there was another time, just before Christmas, when Fred had brought Herb to school. He'd rolled down his car window and shouted to Teddy, *Merry Christmas.* And Teddy had said it back to him. And they'd smiled big and exchanged waves. But all that was before his adulterous mother had killed his stepfather.

It was two or three cigarettes later that the door opened and Fred came out followed by Agnes and then the sheriff. The moon, half full, had gotten higher and the stars seemed brighter now. In that meager light, Teddy saw it before the little procession got to where he and Pete stood. His mother, head bowed, was more round shouldered than he ever recalled her being. And then about the same time as he heard her sobbing, he saw the handcuffs. Teddy blurted out, not caring if the sheriff heard him, "Shit, Pete, he's treatin' her like she's a gangster."

Pete, mindful of being a paroled convict, came back barely above a whisper, "She killed a man, Teddy."

"He had it comin'."

Looking at the approaching trio, Pete said nothing.

"We're gonna go out to the ranch," said the sheriff to Pete. "I'll need to visit with you more at the crime scene. It seems that Mrs. Kinney and Mr. Phillips have a slightly different version of what happened."

Pete's heart jumped into his throat. Anger launched the words from his tongue. "How's that?"

Agnes cried, "I warned him, Pete. I begged him to stop. He just wouldn't. I didn't have a choice. He would've killed George."

Pete snorted. "That's not how you said it happened when I got there."

"You misunderstood. I was really upset. Maybe I wasn't making myself clear."

Pete shook his head. "Well, I guess if that's your story now, so be it. I just told what I heard you say."

And then the sobbing went away, and her voice cleared. "Well, did you tell the sheriff that you and I don't get along? That you've got it out for me. Or did you leave that part out?"

"I've got nothing against you, Agnes. That's all in your mind."

"Bullshit."

Fred's head swiveled side to side several times in apparent disgust. It caused Teddy to recall that Herb had told him his father was a Mormon bishop. His anger was replaced by shame. It was like Fred had God on his side and Teddy had nobody, not even Pete. If he'd just told the same as his mother and George this wouldn't be happening. She wouldn't be in handcuffs.

The sheriff took a hold of Agnes' left arm and moved on. "We'll sort this out later. My deputy and the highway patrol are waitin' for us at the ranch."

Agnes got in the sheriff's pickup. She had started to quietly cry again, the inescapable reality of the trouble she was in having gripped her. In her mind she couldn't let go of the cold mean-spirited image she had of Tom. For the past year whenever she thought of him it wasn't in a loving way. No, they had a love-less marriage and she'd escaped, found something good and then here he comes to spoil it. *What an asshole. He deserved what he got.*

A chain attached to an eye bolt in the floorboard lay between Agnes' feet. The sheriff, probably a little older than George, picked it up with his boney hands. "I'm gonna hook this to your handcuffs."

Agnes whimpered. "Please, that ain't necessary. I'll be good."

"Sorry, it's policy." He clipped the floor chain to the chain that ran between the cuffs leaving her unable to raise her hands.

The sheriff started out of the parking lot, the others following. Agnes sat quietly, crying. They'd cleaned her face and removed the tissue from her nose that was cracked but not broken. Anger, hatred welled up within her as she tasted the saltiness of her tears and snot unable to wipe them away.

CHAPTER SEVENTEEN

As dreams are wont to do, they often turn into nightmares. And so it was with Agnes, her dream, her fantasy of one day becoming Mrs. George Phillips, a respectable rancher's wife, had blown up. Turned sour just like everything else in her life. All on account of Tom Kinney and Pete.

They went over and over again what happened at the ranch. The sheriff intent on trying to trip her up on her version of things. When at last they were done, and Tom was loaded into the hearse and Agnes was hopeful that the sheriff would change his mind, he said, *self-defense just don't wash with your husband being shot in the back.*

Since Sunday night, the day of the shooting, Tom had been at Fred Snyder's funeral home and Agnes in the Elkhorn County jail charged with voluntary manslaughter. George, on the other hand, was still in the hospital with broken and cracked ribs, a broken nose, two missing teeth and a concussion. It now being Wednesday there were a number of people upset with the entire mess, among them was Teddy.

"Son, your uncle's right. You better go to school," said Frank as he carved out a piece of sourdough hotcake and put it in his mouth. He chewed a couple of times before adding, "If ya don't, you'll end up being a dumb shit like me." The other men at the table laughed as if to validate his self-deprecation.

Teddy came back. "You saw yesterday's paper."

"So?"

"So, everybody at school will know my mother was sleeping around and because of it she killed my step-father."

Pete, who was standing at the stove cooking more hotcakes, cut in, "You can't just hole up out here. You said yourself the principal threatened to sic the truancy officer on you if you missed any more school. You don't want to tangle with him."

Old Charlie, having been sober and clear eyed for a good while now, chimed in, "That's a true story, son. With your ma likely taking up residence in Deerlodge, he'll send your ass to reform school."

Teddy sighed. "It don't matter anyway. I ain't got no place to live."

Charlie looked over at Pete while Teddy didn't bother. No one suggested the obvious. Finally. Pete said, "You might have to go live with your grandma in Kansas."

Teddy scoffed. "She don't want me."

"How do you know?"

Teddy thought of the letter his mother hadn't had the nerve to mail. "I know. Besides, in a couple months I'll be sixteen and I can be on my own."

"Too bad you ain't older," said Frank. "You could join the service. That's what I did."

Pete looked at the clock on the wall beyond Teddy. "Well, if you're going to school you better head out for the bus stop."

Teddy came back quick, his tone sharp. "I ain't going."

Pete frowned. "Alright then, the wood box is about empty and I'm gonna need help cleaning up here. Lots a dishes to wash and dry."

"Fine with me," said Teddy as he pushed his chair back.

Frank threw in, mostly to ease the tension in the room, "Pete, you make a passable cook." And then he added, "But that ain't saying I'd be opposed to pitching in to bail Agnes out." Everybody laughed except Teddy.

During their trip to town yesterday, Pete and Teddy had learned several things. One was that George was being released from the hospital around ten or eleven this morning. And two was Agnes' bail was $1,000. And three was, she wanted out of jail bad.

They parked where cars usually did and went in the front door like most people passing by the counter with a nod and *good morning* to the old lady behind it and on down the hall towards room #5. They were not quite to George's open door when a woman's voice, caustic and hateful, stopped them in their tracks. She said, "You're not bailing that slut out. She's brought enough embarrassment to this family." The voice paused before hurling the words at George, "Don't you have any respect for mother?"

There was momentary silence before George fired back. "You don't sit out there alone in that big house night after night. You busted your ass to be gone from this place as soon as you could. So, you're welcome for that education and nice big city life over there in Billings."

"Don't play that card with me, Dad. I've told you a number of times how much I appreciate all that you've done for me. But this woman, she's married or was until she killed the guy."

"You've never met her. You don't even know her."

"I've heard rumors. She gets around."

"All you've heard is just gossip."

"Gossip doesn't come from thin air."

"People like to grow it to ward off boredom."

"Well, some old men like to do other things to ward off boredom."

"Don't get a smart mouth with me."

"I've got to go, but just understand if you bail this woman out and carry on with her, you'll never see me or your grandson again."

"That's not fair, Beth."

The young red-haired woman suddenly exited George's room breezing on by Pete and Teddy her high heels clicking down the tiled hallway. Teddy watched her go, dressed nice and all. The look of money. *What could that bitch know about Ma? She's never had to live over the Lariat Bar.* He followed Pete inside. The look on their faces gave them away.

George said, "You heard?"

Pete nodded. "Couldn't help it."

To his credit, George's face showed remorse. "You know I can't go to the jail."

Pete said what keeping his job required, "Yeah, I reckon you don't have much choice."

"No. I don't. You heard how she was."

Teddy wanted in the worst way to take up his mother's side of things. It wasn't all her fault. George had been the one to come by the cook shack between meals to see if, *she needed anything.* From there he'd sweetened the pot in a none too subtle way. And now, here he was conveniently forgetting that it could have been him over at Snyder's funeral home had Agnes not pulled the trigger on Tom. He was turning his back on her for those brief visits from his daughter on holidays and his birthday. Teddy hoped on the other 360 days that he was lonely as hell.

CHAPTER EIGHTEEN

The three of them squeezed into the cab of George's pickup with Pete behind the wheel. They were sitting uncomfortably close given the tension that existed for leaving Agnes in jail. Pete and Teddy both knew that she would be expecting them to come today with George and his checkbook to bail her out. Instead, they started for the ranch without anyone suggesting they stop by the jail and at least tell Agnes she wasn't getting out.

They rode the entire way home listening to the radio with some occasional "fluff talk", *hopefully, winter will be over by July so we can cut some hay*, or *this old truck handles the snow purty good*. But nobody said a word about Agnes until Pete parked in front of George's house and they'd gotten out. It was still awkward between them.

Pete said, "Need some help gettin' in the house?"

George hesitated, glanced at Teddy, and then said, "Yeah, help me to the door."

George turned, saying nothing to Teddy and started to gingerly negotiate the rutted snow with Pete's help. When they reached the door, Pete said in a normal voice that Teddy could hear, "You got 'er from here?"

Teddy saw George nod then the two of them went to whispering, looking intently at one another until George abruptly broke it off with words Teddy could hear. "Tell him."

It wasn't until they were in Pete's pickup and backing around to leave that Teddy asked, "What was that about?"

Pete sighed. "He wants you gone."

A hurt look came to Teddy's face. "When?"

"Soon. Next week."

"Next week! I can't-"

"I know, I know, we'll figure something out."

Teddy snorted, fully aware of his options. "What? You know I ain't got anywhere to go."

Pete stopped in front of the cook shack and turned the truck's engine off. He made no effort to move, shaking his head instead. "Even if Agnes was to get out of jail, Beth doesn't want her here."

"You think they're gonna let her out?"

Pete shook his head. "No, she'd be smart to cut a deal if they'll give her one."

"You think they will?"

"Don't know. Maybe if she quits lyin', tells them how sorry she is. It blows prosecutor's egos way up when they can get somebody to beg for their freedom."

Quiet overtook them. An answer to Teddy's dilemma still not forthcoming. Finally, he said, looking Pete in the eyes so as to apply maximum guilt, "You know, you could fix this."

"Fix what?"

"Me having a place to stay."

"How's that?"

"You could sign for me to join the Marines."

"Only a parent can do that."

"Cut the crap, Pete. You're big on my mother being honest. How about you?"

Pete laughed nervously and shook his head while staring down through the steering wheel.

Teddy came again, anger in his voice. "Would it be that bad to admit I'm your son? Are you ashamed of me or are you afraid it's gonna cost you?"

"I don't know. Look at what a mess I've made of my life."

"This will be all I ever ask of you, Pete."

"We'd have to lie about your age."

"If we don't, I'll be on the street."

"And if we're caught and they want to be hardnosed about it, I could go back to Deerlodge."

"For that?"

"It's breaking the law."

"I'm sorry. I know it's a lot to ask. If you do it, I promise, I'll be outta your life for good."

Pete remained quiet for a few seconds, still staring at the floorboard and then abruptly reached for the doorhandle. "Let me think about it."

They went inside. Pete stoked the fire and set the big pot of beans and bacon that he'd prepared for supper that morning on the stove. He was matter of fact. It was like their conversation in the pickup, or even their trip to town, hadn't taken place. And then, as if to distance himself even further from those events he said, "You got some old grungy clothes? Something you won't mind getting' paint and sheep shit on?"

Teddy snorted. "A lot of my clothes would fall into that category."

Pete came back straight faced. "Put 'em on. You can help us brand this afternoon."

They drove over to where the sheep were located, going up an alley bounded by half acre pens defined by woven wire and two strands of barbed all stapled to wooden posts. The ewes with the oldest lambs, the ones that had already been docked and branded were here. After three sets of these they came to another east-west alley and the sun sheds. Frank was already there standing beside a waist high pile of hay bales. A yellow can of paint and a stubby branding iron, maybe a foot long, was lying next to the can. Frank laughed and called out, "I see ya found yourself a catcher."

"Yeah, he'll be wishing he'd gone to school."

Frank laughed. He said, unaware of how it had gone in town, "No offense, Pete, but I'm lookin' forward to eatin' Agnes' chuck tonight."

Pete came back quick. "Sorry, you're gonna have to put up with mine again."

"Well, what happened? I thought you was retrievin' both her and George today."

"It's a long story." Pete went on quick. "Frank, you brand. I'll dock and castrate. Teddy, you catch the lambs. Alright?"

Teddy nodded and climbed over the four foot high panel into the pen. Pete did not return Frank's questioning look as he followed Teddy into the pen. There were four ewes and four lambs all crowded under the shed portion of the pen. Teddy snatched up a lamb and brought it to Pete who was on his knees in the mud and manure.

"Hold him so I can get at his tail."

Teddy dropped to his knees. Cold manure instantly penetrated the hole in his pants. He could feel the wetness engulf his knees.

"Hold him still, Teddy."

Teddy applied a tighter grip on the lamb that faced him. He watched as Pete squeezed the handles of the plier-like elastrator expanding the thick rubber ring and slid it up the lamb's tail so as to leave the lamb with a bob of about three inches when the longer part fell off. He then grabbed another rubber ring and fit it over the four prongs of the elastrator. "Put him on his back."

Teddy turned the lamb over and right away was taken aback to the point he wanted to let it go. Its belly was alive with ticks. "Shit, Pete, look at that."

Pete ignored Teddy's queasiness and reached for the lamb's scrotum. "Hold him tight, Teddy. Don't wanna be pinching a nut."

Teddy cringed as Pete slid the rubber ring over the lamb's scrotum and released it.

Pete said, "Alright pick him up. Hold him tight against you with his left side facing Frank."

Teddy reluctantly complied and stepped close to the panel so Frank could brand the lamb. The brand, called 7 Timbers, consisted of crossed sticks resembling what Teddy thought looked like a teepee with a 7 inside it, was dripping heavy red paint. A stringer of it landed on Teddy's sweatshirt and the upper part of his jeans. Frank laughed. "Might as well get that over with on the first one."

Teddy looked down at the paint on his clothes and the mud and manure on his pants. He'd barely had time to process that image when he spotted three ticks on the stomach area of his sweatshirt. It was instant disgust that caused him to brush at them in a frantic way. Pete and Frank began to laugh and then they laughed harder when Teddy saw another tick on the back of his puffy green glove. He shrieked, almost like a girl, "Shit, these damned ticks are everywhere."

And then Pete quit laughing. His voice became stern. "Well, you're the one that wants to quit school. Here's what you get."

"Not to do this."

"Get that Marine nonsense out of your head."

"I got no place to go, Pete. You don't want me. Nobody does."

Pete sighed and shook his head. He wanted to disagree but couldn't find words for it. "Let's just get on with what we got to do."

Like he had to remind them of where they were in life, Teddy said. "We can't even take a shower tonight."

Frank, half serious but mostly trying to bleed off the tension between them, laughed and said, "Another month the ice 'll be off the crik and we can clean up then." He laughed some more. Pete and Teddy remained stone-faced locked onto one another.

Pete said, knowing that it wouldn't appease what ailed Teddy, "You got that metal tub in your ma's room. Heat up some water tonight. Take a bath."

Teddy scoffed. "Two-hour process to take a lukewarm bath."

And then Pete's frustration with it all boiled over. He was madder at himself than he was Teddy. Nonetheless, he said, loud and sarcastic, "Well, why don't you just hike your young ass up to George's tonight and see if he'll let you take a shower there?"

Teddy shot back, quick as a rattlesnake strikes. "Screw you, Pete." He then climbed out of the pen and started for the cookshack. Pete did not go after him.

CHAPTER NINETEEN

Teddy did not go to supper, simple as it was, beans, biscuits and coffee. He was ashamed of how he'd behaved that afternoon. From where he lay on his mother's bed he could hear Charlie, who'd replaced him as lamb catcher, complaining about his aching back. "I'm gittin' too old for this shit."

Frank laughed and pointed to Charlie's shirt sleeve. "I see ya brought one a your friends with you."

Charlie's eyes searched where Frank was pointing. "Sonovabitch, I been pluckin' them things off me all afternoon."

A big smile came to Frank's face. "Well, at least you won't be sleepin' alone tonight." Everybody at the table, but Charlie, laughed.

It was Fred, normally quiet but unaware of what had happened at the sun sheds who called out the obvious. "So, where's Teddy tonight?"

The question had been mostly directed at Pete. He was still formulating a white lie to explain Teddy's absence when, maybe due to the ticks and his aching muscles, Charlie blurted out, "He's moping in the back room."

Pete, knowing that Teddy had likely heard. frowned in Charlie's direction. He thought to come back with, *Teddy ain't feelin' good.* Fear of Charlie calling him on that and saying how it was the oldest hand on the place came to be lamb catcher today kept him mute. Meanwhile Fred and Eddy, ignorant of that afternoon's events, sat suspicious knowing that Charlie would fill them in later.

Not long after all the men but Pete had left, Teddy came out. Pete was clearing the table. Teddy caught his eye. "I'm sorry about today."

Pete shook his head. "It wasn't good."

"I know. I shouldn't have done that."

"Charlie will make sure everybody knows what happened. If you was to stay here you'd be a long time diggin' yourself outta that hole."

Teddy's eyes got watery. Before he could speak, Pete said, almost indifferently, "You know you pull a stunt like today in the Corps and they'll throw your ass in the brig."

Teddy's face torqued up into a look of desperate anguish. "I know, Pete. I'd know better in the Marines."

Pete snorted and laughed derisively. "You damned sure would." He paused and then added, "Can I trust you to finish cleaning up here? I'm going over to George's."

"You think he knows about today?"

Pete shrugged. "Doesn't matter. His mind is made up on your account."

After Pete left, Teddy ate the supper that he'd been too ashamed to come out and eat when the hired hands were there. It tasted good to him as he was ravenous and possibly the fact that Pete had worked in the prison kitchen for much of his ten years there.

He'd gone the extra mile in cleaning up the kitchen. It was as tidy as if his mother had done it. In a way the evening was like they had gotten to be when Agnes was there. She'd go to George's right after supper, and he'd earn his keep cleaning up.

It was not so dark outside that you needed a light to see, but close to it, when Pete came back from George's. Teddy was sitting on the couch listening to Ernest Tubb sing *Walking The Floor Over You* when he saw Pete's outline go by the window above the sink. Seconds later the door opened and he stuck his head inside. His eyes made a quick inspection of the room. It appeared he was going to compliment Teddy, instead he said, "We're going to town tomorrow. Right after breakfast."

Teddy thought to ask, *what for?* But Pete was already starting to close the door. He said, barely audible over the radio, "Alright."

CHAPTER TWENTY

In an effort to redeem himself, Teddy got up early and stoked the fire, made coffee and set the table all before Pete got there at 5:00 a.m. He stepped inside, looked around, and said, "You must a got up with the chickens." And then he sat on the chair by the door and began unbuckling his overshoes. He went on while fumbling with one of his buckles, "George said I got till a week from today to find you a new home."

Teddy's stomach began to churn. "What an asshole."

Pete struggled momentarily with the overshoe before it came off. "It's his place."

"You on his side?"

"Well, he ain't running an orphanage."

"So, what are we gonna do?"

Pete stood up and looked hard at Teddy. "*We*, are going to Bozeman."

"What for?"

"Probably to get in trouble."

At breakfast, Pete lied and told the others that he would be gone a couple of days to take Teddy to his grandma's place in Idaho. All of the men except Charlie wished him good luck. Teddy knew enough to keep his mouth shut and play along even though it bothered him that Charlie wouldn't look at him.

When they had finished doing the breakfast dishes and it was nearly time to go, Teddy asked, "What should I take to Bozeman?"

Pete kept on wiping the counter down. "Just your toilet kit."

"I don't have a proper one."

Pete looked over at him. "A toilet kit?"

"Not one of those fancy zip up things. I keep my stuff in a paper bag in my suitcase."

Pete sighed. "I've got a shoe box and a string that I'll give you."

"Thanks, I appreciate that, Pete."

Pete scoffed and tossed his head slightly like he was drawing attention to Teddy's pathetic circumstances. Little did Teddy know, the shoe box, courtesy of the Montana State Penitentiary, held Pete's toilet kit.

Teddy came back. "So, I take it you're gonna help me get in the Marines?"

"It's against my better judgement but I don't know what else to do with you."

"It's what I want, Pete. It'll work out, you'll see."

Pete sighed deeply. "I guess we will."

It bothered Teddy that Pete had so little confidence in him to make it in the Marines. On the way to town this concern grew into a full-blown worry that took over his mind. The Naysayer within him pointed repeatedly to him being grossed out by the sheep ticks and quitting. At the time, it had seemed like the right thing to do. And then the Naysayer's voice became sarcastic, cruel almost, *now, this same kid wants to go off to war and fight the Japs. What a joke.*

At a quarter past nine, Pete parked his pickup in front of the Elkhorn County courthouse. To either side of its steps were large posters suspended in iron frame stands that depicted patriotic enticements for the various branches of the military. The Marine poster was of a guy in a dress blue uniform on the deck of a navy ship. Patches of grass peppered the largely snow-covered ground. Teddy said, his heart having kicked into high gear, "We going to see the recruiter now?"

Pete reached for his doorhandle. "No, your mother."

"Oh."

"You do want to see her before you leave, don't you?"

To be honest, Teddy hadn't thought that much about seeing his mother before he left. Her being in jail made it different somehow. He generalized, *nothing in my life is ever like normal people's lives.* Pulses of anger and shame crossed his mind. He said, aloud, "Sure, Pete."

They climbed the steps and went through the mostly glass door. Immediately to their right were stairs going to the basement. A sign above them read: SHERIFF'S OFFICE/ COUNTY JAIL. At the bottom of the stairs was an open door. A middle-aged woman with dark hair was standing behind the counter inside.

"Can I help you?"

Pete rested his forearms lightly on the counter. "Yeah, we'd like to see Agnes Walker."

The woman shook her head. "Well, I don't know. Visiting hours aren't until three o'clock."

"Be any chance you could make an exception? Her son here is on his way out of town to go in the service."

From an open door to the right of the woman came a voice. "It's alright, Gladys, I'll take'em back." Moments later the sheriff stepped out of his office. Upon seeing who it was he ginned up a fake smile. "Mr. Walker, I was thinkin' of coming to visit you today."

"How's that?"

"Got a call from your parole officer. Seems a little country store north of Billings was robbed last night. The store owner said your picture sure looked like the fella that did it."

Pete's bowels began to roll. "That's bullshit, Sheriff. I was at the ranch last night. Mr. Phillips will testify to that."

The Sheriff laughed briefly at the anguish he was causing Pete. "I figured as much. Told your P.O. that but he wanted me to check you out. And whaddaya know, you saved me a trip."

"Well, I aim to please."

The Sheriff glanced at Teddy and then back to Pete. "Did I hear you say the boy is going into the service?"

Regret at mentioning it to Gladys swept over Pete. "Yeah."

"Jumping the gun isn't he?"

"His mother 'll have to sign for him."

Teddy suddenly became weak kneed as the Sheriff began visually aging him like he was a farm animal. A grin began to grow on his face until finally he said, "Well, good luck to ya."

They went through a door beyond Gladys that emptied into a hallway. It was a no frills facility. A bare cement floor and cinder block walls painted yellow between each of the five cells defined it. The last cell to the right was designated for female prisoners. "Here ya are," said the Sheriff, "You got ten minutes."

Agnes was laying on her bed. She sat up. Her face shouted out the stress of jail life and worry that her future held even more of it. "I thought you were coming yesterday."

Pete waited for the office door to close behind the sheriff and then looked at Agnes. He sighed. "Ain't no easy way to say it. George isn't gonna go your bail."

Genuine surprise swam to the surface of her sunken eyes. "Why the hell not?"

"Beth won't allow it."

"That spoilt bitch. What's it to her?"

"I guess she doesn't want you taking her mama's place."

Agnes scoffed. "So, George just becomes a monk?"

"She's threatening him with never seeing her or his grandson."

"And George caved into her?"

Pete was silent for a few seconds before twisting the knife. "She wants Teddy off the place too."

It was a tsunami of rage followed by hurt such that it staggered Agnes to the point she clutched the bars of the cell door and bowed her head. She began to cry, saying nothing. She'd given herself to George thinking he was different, that her ship had come in.

And then Pete twisted the knife one more time. "Teddy wants to join the Marines. I'd like your blessing."

Agnes instantly looked up. "No, no way in hell am I agreeing to that."

Teddy cut in, "I've got no place to go, Ma."

"You can go to your grandma's."

"You know that won't work."

"I'll call her. I'll write her. I'll make her do it."

Teddy snorted. "Grandma's not gonna do anything she doesn't want to."

"We don't have the time," said Pete, "to argue with that old woman."

Agnes instantly glared at him. "Then why don't you man-up and take care of your son?"

Teddy looked at Pete, hopeful of what he would say. It was not to be. "That's wishful thinking on your part. Besides, what can I offer him?"

Agnes looked incredulous. She shrieked, "A place to live."

"I'd have to move on, find another job. Not everybody wants an ex-con who is on parole."

Agnes began to silently cry again. Tears streaming down her face and snuffling frequently she reached through the bars with her left hand and touched Teddy's cheek. "I guess we'll be going our separate ways."

Teddy felt like he might cry too and then the feeling went away. He didn't want to think that he'd become numb to his mother's affection. It appeared though, with all the bouncing around from one dead end job to another and men that, even young as he was, he knew weren't going to last, had taken its toll. He said, "I'll write you."

And then Pete said, "I guess we better be goin' 'fore the sheriff comes an' rousts us out."

Agnes, her hand still through the bars, squeezed Teddy's shoulder, "You be careful."

Teddy nodded knowing that was as close to saying, *I love you,* as she was likely to get. He did not want to make it awkward for her so he said, "We'll be seeing ya, Ma."

They then walked away not coming back or even slowing in response to Agnes' sobbing. As they went past Gladys' desk she called out from her normal world, "Have a good day."

Teddy's mind exploded. *My mother is in your jail for murder and I'm being evicted from my latest home to go off and fight the Japs.* It was a struggle to drain off the sarcasm before he said, "You have a nice day too."

It was yet another embarrassment for Teddy to go by the school and formally withdraw. He'd not wanted to as he was certain that he'd see people that knew him and his situation. Pete, on the other hand, had said Teddy couldn't just stop showing up. *They'll sic the truancy officer on you. And if you do make it into the Marines, you don't want that guy pokin' around cuz he damned sure knows how old you are.* Nonetheless, when Teddy saw Becky and a couple of her normal Mormon girlfriends he wanted in the worst way to say to them that he was off to the Marines instead of grandma's house. As it was, he turned away and said nothing.

CHAPTER TWENTY-ONE

Pete checked his watch yet again. It was 10:15 and they were already five or so miles down the road to Bozeman. Dodging a pothole that had come with the spring thaw, he said, "If my buddy's there, I'm hoping we can make this happen pretty quick."

Teddy had been suspicious of Pete's apparent confidence that things would go smooth with the recruiter. He probed, "The recruiter is your friend?"

Pete's face took on a more serious look. "He owes me."

"Owes you?"

"I saved his life."

"During the war?"

Pete looked to be going back in time. "He was wounded. Laying out there in the open. Workin' on bleedin' out and he knew it. Krauts had us pretty well pinned down. For a time, Windy stayed mostly quiet. Trying to play dead, I guess. But then it was like Windy got scared and he started to cry. I-"

Teddy cut in, a grin on his face, "Windy, that was the guy's name?"

Pete nodded. "That's what we called him. Wendell Barnes was his real name."

"Oh, did he mind being called, Windy?"

"Lots of guys in the Corps get nicknames, usually cuz they're liked. In Windy's case, not so much."

It then came to Teddy that he'd derailed Pete in telling the story. He said, "Sorry, didn't mean to interrupt."

Pete went on. "Well, long story short is I couldn't take the crying so I all of a sudden jumped up and started running for Windy. It was like I lost control of myself. Lucky for me, the guys laid down a pretty good covering fire or else I would have ended up Swiss cheese."

"So did ya get shot?"

Pete looked briefly at Teddy like he was an idiot. "Well, hell yeah, I got shot, twice. Didn't your mother ever tell you any of this?"

That day on the school bus when Jimmy Polson had told him how Pete accosted his mother came back to Teddy. And how the only thing that prevented his father from going to the sheriff and Pete going back to Deerlodge was George pleading Pete's war record. Teddy feigned ignorance. "This is the first I've ever heard about you being in the war."

Pete snorted. "Figures, your ma 's never got anything good to say about me."

Teddy tucked away all the bad that Jimmy had told him and went on. "So, did they give you a medal for saving Windy?"

The old Pete, the blow and go Pete before Agnes killed Tom and went to jail, had seemingly been on vacation since all of that had happened. But now here he was, sans any modesty. "Hell yeah, they did. It was a big deal. I got a purple heart and silver star. Some general, I don't remember his name, pinned 'em on me in front of everybody over there in France. Had the whole battalion out there lined up. It was quite a deal."

"Sounds like it."

"Oh yeah, it was in all the papers." He paused and laughed. "I got more free drinks and tail than any two grown men can handle." And then he laughed again.

Teddy brought Pete back to the moment. "So, you reckon Windy is going to help us out?"

Pete got serious. "He damned well better."

CHAPTER TWENTY-TWO

Because of the need to conserve gas for the war, the government had decreed that no one was to drive faster than 45 miles per hour. Consequently, they did not arrive at the federal building in Bozeman until a few minutes till one. As he looked up at the big white stone structure, a swarm of butterflies settled in Teddy's stomach. There was a part of him that hoped Windy wasn't there and that the whole thing would fall through. And then the reality of his miserable life smacked him in the face. *So, what would you do then*? He wished that he had options like his friend Jimmy.

Just inside the door, hanging on the wall, was a directory. Teddy read from it. "Marines are in room 2C."

"Hopefully, they're back from noon chow," said Pete.

As they started towards the stairs, Teddy said, the demons of doubt working hard on him, "You think Windy will remember you?"

Pete did not break stride. "I ain't gonna give him that choice."

At the top of the stairs was a good-sized waiting area with heavy oak chairs that lacked any padding. To the left were two offices, the Marines in one and the Navy in the other. To the right was the Army. Straight ahead was a hallway. From the directory downstairs Teddy knew it likely led to the U.S. Department of Agriculture. The doors to the Navy and Army were both open, kept that way by wedges of wood jammed under their bottoms. The Marines' office, however, was dark and locked. Pete stuck his head in the Navy's office. "Your pal next door come to work today?"

A sailor with salt and pepper hair in a meticulously pressed white uniform was sitting behind a big wooden desk. He looked up from what he was working on. "He's here. Just running late from chow, I guess."

Pete frowned. "Figures."

The sailor stood up. "Maybe I can help you."

Pete scoffed. "No, the boy here doesn't wanna be a swabbe."

The sailor flashed Pete a sour look. "I guess you can wait out there then."

Pete turned away nearly bumping into Teddy who had been eyeing the sailor's uniform. "Let's go sit down."

Teddy hesitated. "Maybe we should at least talk to this guy."

Pete looked Teddy hard in the eyes, his voice echoing in the cavernous area. "You know, coming over here has caused me to use my entire gas ration for the month. And now you pull this." He paused and shook his head. Lowering his voice, knowing the Navy recruiter was all ears, he added, "You know what we're up against here. So, if you want my help, it's the Marines or you're on your own."

"Sorry, Pete."

"Let's go sit down."

They took seats against the wall beneath a painting of General Custer with long hair dressed in buckskins. Without fail, every time Teddy saw a picture of Custer he wondered how a man could have been so stupid. And then his mind took off considering the likelihood of a Custer type being in charge of him and that he could end up like those poor guys at the Little Bighorn. His imagination was in high gear with him about to be bayoneted by an enraged Jap when he heard footsteps clicking up the stairs. He shifted his attention to the sound. Like a car jack, the owner of the footsteps revealed himself: the top of his head, his clean-shaven face, a few colorful ribbons on a dark green uniform, a leather belt, matching trousers and finally, highly polished shoes. The man stopped. Before he could rein it in, concern escaped to his eyes. And then he recovered, forced a smile and began walking towards Pete and Teddy.

Pete stood and extended his hand. "Long time no see, no hear, no nuthin'."

Windy shook Pete's hand. He laughed in a brief and uneasy way. "You know how it is, outta sight outta mind."

"Yeah, ten years at Deerlodge will get a person dropped off most people's Christmas card list."

Pete's voice was loud, like the usual Pete. It bounced off the black tile floor and the flowery wallpaper. Teddy cringed and swiveled his head at the Navy and then the Army recruiters. They'd both picked up on Pete's reference to doing time in prison.

Windy started walking. "Let's go to my office."

Noting the stripes on Windy's sleeve, Pete said, "See ya made Gunny."

Windy keyed the lock and opened the door. He snorted. "Finally, last year."

They sat down, Windy behind the desk, Pete and Teddy straight out from it. In the next instant, however, Windy stood back up and stuck his hand out to Teddy. "Gunnery Sergeant Wendell Barnes."

Teddy stood and shook his hand. "Teddy Walker, Sir."

A smile came to Windy's face and then went away as fast as it had appeared. Still standing, he said, "Pete your uncle?"

An awkward silence descended on the room. Teddy looked at Pete to break it. It appeared he was about to do that when the Navy recruiter walked slowly by their open door on his way to the drinking fountain. Pete mumbled as he got up, "Big ears." He closed the door and looked at Windy.

"I'm the boy's father, but that ain't what it says on his birth certificate."

Windy kept a sober look and nodded. "So, what's your purpose in being here today?"

"Teddy wants to sign up for the Corps."

Windy glanced at Teddy and said, like he wasn't even there. "Not a problem if he's old enough."

"He's seventeen," said Pete.

"That's good, but he'll still need proof and a parent's signature on the consent form."

Pete went quiet, staring at Windy before finally saying, "I'll sign the form, but you know I ain't got no birth certificate."

Windy sighed. "I'm sorry Pete. You know the Corps and their rules." He then shook out a cigarette from a pack of Camels, without offering Pete one, and lit it. He took a draw on the cigarette like the matter was finished and exhaled the smoke clouding the space between him and Pete.

It was obvious to Teddy that Windy was a poor judge of character, at least Pete's he was. He added, "Why don't you just have the boy's mother come with the birth certificate and she can sign?"

Pete snapped. "You little prick. Why are you being so chickenshit about this?"

To his credit, Windy had the good sense to show some fear as Pete was a head taller and probably forty pounds heavier than him. Nonetheless, his fear did not influence his response in the way Pete had hoped or Teddy had thought it would. He said, pointing his smoldering Camel at Pete, "Listen Walker, I owe you for France. So, thank you. But what you're asking is too much. I'm eligible for retirement. I can't risk it by knowingly taking a fraudulent enlistment. I just can't do it."

Pete snorted and leaned back in his chair. "Shudda let the Krauts finish you off."

"You're too good of a Marine to do that."

"Don't blow smoke up my ass."

Windy sighed. The conversation was sounding like a prelude to a bar room fight. He said, "Maybe you and Teddy should just go on home now. Come back when he's old enough."

Teddy chimed in. "I don't have a home."

Windy looked at him and then Pete, his expression one of bewilderment. "I'm sorry." He did not probe the situation, his eyes suggesting that he wished it would go away. He took another draw on his cigarette.

Out of the blue, Pete played his trump card. He said coyly, "Whaddaya hear from Susan these days?"

Fear returned to Windy's face. "Susan?"

Pete laughed sarcastically. "Yeah, your sister, Susan. The one that used to turn two dollar tricks in Denver."

"You bastard. Leave her out of this. She's got a good life now."

"Oh, I know. I looked her up right after I got out of the pen. Had lots of time to think about her. But she's too good now for trash like me what with kids, a nice house and that big shot banker husband of hers."

Teddy looked over at Pete. "This ain't right."

Pete shook his head. "Well, if he don't let you in the Corps where do you think you're going to sleep tonight? Or for that matter, what are you going to eat? You want me to quit Phillips and you and me go on the road with no money. *Oh, by the way would you like to hire an ex-con? My parole officer will vouch for me.* How 'bout you Windy? The Corps lookin' for any felons?"

It went quiet again, the three of them assessing one another like they were in a poker game. Windy's cigarette hand rested on the desk in front of him. Smoke, rising up from it was the only movement amongst them. Finally, Windy said, "You'd really ruin my sister's life, wouldn't you?"

"If that's what it takes to give Teddy one, I would."

Windy shook his head. "You're a real prize, Walker."

CHAPTER TWENTY-THREE

The General Sherman Hotel was four stories high. It was downtown, not far from where the military conducted their physicals. All of the men stayed there the night before their exam.

Pete stopped his old truck under the hotel canopy as if he was a paying guest. Teddy knew that it was unlikely he would come in, but he asked anyway. "Gonna stick around for supper?"

"Naw, you know I'm broke."

"Sorry."

Pete laughed. "I was broke long before you came along. It's kind of a permanent condition with me."

Teddy smiled briefly before looking at his toilet kit in the shoebox on the seat between them. His expression became almost fearful. "I'll write ya if you want."

Pete was leaning slightly forward with the fingers of his hands laced together on the top of the steering wheel. His eyes appeared fixated on a cart piled high with suitcases and garment bags. "It boggles the mind, don't it, that anybody would need that much shit to take a trip?"

Teddy nodded, mindful of Pete having ignored what he'd just said. He went along. "Yeah, it does. Don't see why they need so many clothes."

"Ah hell, Teddy. Some people change their clothes half dozen times a day. In their minds they ain't presentable if they don't." He paused and snorted a laugh. "Can you imagine going to one of these folks' house with a little sheep-shit on your boots?"

Teddy laughed, recalling that he'd smelled it more than once at supper in the cook shack. And then, while the both of them had receding laughs on their faces, a big black Packard pulled in behind Pete's dented truck with a short jag of hay in the back. He glanced at his rearview mirror. "Speakin' of the Vanderbilts, I guess I better skedaddle."

Teddy reached for the shoebox and slid it across the seat before picking it up. Pete noted it but said nothing to deal with the white elephant in the cab. Teddy moved on, working the handle and pushing the door part way open. "Well, thanks for everything, Pete."

Pete looked again at the Packard in his mirror while lighting a cigarette. Cold air from the open door rushed in and the Packard tooted its horn as Pete gestured at Teddy with the two fingers that held the Lucky Strike. "Pay attention. Keep your mouth shut and do what you're told and you'll be alright."

Teddy sensed there was a different Pete trying to come out and then, in the next instant, the Packard laid on his horn. "I better go, Pete." Teddy slammed the door and started with his shoebox past the big cart with the bags. Suddenly, from behind him he heard Pete call out, "Teddy."

Teddy turned around. Pete was standing on the driver's side running board looking over the top of his truck's cab. He shouted, "I'm hell on writin' but I do purty good at readin' letters."

Teddy smiled, a feel-good smile. The first in a long time. He waved and the Packard honked again. Pete laughed and drove off.

Because of the heavy foot traffic and the careless attitude of people in closing a door to keep the cold air out, the General Sherman had two of them about six feet apart.

The bottom halves were dark cherry wood and the top halves clear glass. Teddy pushed through the second door into the lobby. He was immediately taken aback by its opulence. A crystal chandelier overhead and to his left a huge rock fireplace, its lively flames crackling an invitation to sit in the padded chairs in front of it. And keeping watch on those who did was a bull elk. Dead ahead was the front desk. A gray-haired man with wire rimmed glasses in a white shirt and dark blue tie stood behind it. He made eye contact with Teddy. "Can I help you, young man?"

Teddy set his shoebox on the counter and removed the lid, exposing its contents to the clerk. He took out the paper that Windy had given him. "I'm supposed to stay here tonight. I'm going into the Marines."

The clerk did a double take. He said, his tone patronizing, "You are, huh?"

Teddy did his best to ignore how the man was being. "Yes Sir."

The man shook his head with a sarcastic grin on his face as he studied Teddy's paper. Finally, he reached for a key from one of the cubby holes on the wall behind him. He handed it to Teddy. "You'll be sharing a room. Did they tell you that?"

"No Sir."

"Well, you are. You're in room 415."

Teddy nodded, "Thank you," and started towards the stairs in the corner of the lobby. He'd gone only a few steps when the clerk called out, "There's an elevator right here."

Teddy turned around. The man was pointing to the other side of the room. "You know you're on the fourth floor."

Teddy had never stayed in a hotel before or ridden in an elevator, nor did he know the significance of the '4' in his room number. His face had turned a little red probably giving him away. "Yes Sir, I know."

The clerk laughed. "Suit yourself but I figure a few days from now you'll be getting all the exercise you can handle."

Teddy started up the stairs. By the time he got to the fourth floor he was breathing hard. It gave him pause. *Shit, I hope the Marines start out easy or I'll be in trouble.* The first room on his right was #401. He continued on down the hall looking right to left until he got to #407 and figured out that #415 would be on the right. Picking up the pace his search took him all the way to the end of the hall. He thought of just unlocking the door and going in but then he thought maybe his roommate might be there and not appreciate him just coming in unannounced. He knocked. Seconds later he heard footsteps and the door opened. An intimidating guy, muscular with dark hair and moustache filled the entrance. He gave Teddy a puzzled look. "What can I do for ya, kid?"

"I'm your roommate."

"My what?"

"I'm going into the Marines."

The guy started to laugh but then caught himself. "Well, alright kid, come on in," There were two beds in the room separated by a nightstand and a lamp. He stopped by the first bed. "I got the bed by the window, so I guess this one is yours."

Teddy set his shoebox on the bed. "Thanks."

The guy snorted. "Don't thank me. The Marines are paying for it."

"Are you going in the Marines too?"

"Yeah, I don't wanna be in any candy-ass outfit."

For a moment Teddy thought to agree with the guy, but he clearly didn't look like a candy-ass and Teddy wasn't certain about himself. So, he said what he thought would give him credibility, "Yeah, my dad was a Marine."

"Was he in the war?"

"Yeah, over in France."

"He kill any Krauts?"

"Yeah, he got shot saving a guy. They gave him a purple heart and the silver star."

"No shit?"

Teddy nodded. "Yeah, he signed for me so I could join early."

"That's pretty swell. What does your mother think about you joining?

It suddenly occurred to Teddy that what credibility he had just generated with this guy, courtesy of Pete, could all be lost if he was to find out that his mother was in jail for murder. To hesitate might cause suspicion. He went all in. "My mother 's dead. She was killed in a car wreck a few years back."

"Oh, sorry to hear that."

Teddy stood there, sucking up the sympathy while at the same time trying to ignore the fact that he was ashamed of his mother. But to have both your parents be felons? He wanted to think that lying about that was ok.

And then the guy offered his hand. "Name's Tony Halverson. I'm from Livingston."

"Teddy Walker, Elkhorn."

Tony's grip had been uncomfortably strong, beyond cordial. He was the man that Teddy wasn't. It was evident that he started thinking as soon as he heard the Walker name. Teddy could see it coming. "You ain't any relative to that woman in the paper that killed her husband here a while back are ya?

A person only gets ambushed when they're caught off guard. The lie slid off Teddy's tongue like warm ice cream. "Oh hell no. Just luck of the draw that we'd have the same last name."

And so it began.

CHAPTER TWENTY-FOUR

Teddy was up early the next morning so that he could shower before breakfast and his physical. It'd been a good while since he'd gone to the bother of heating water and taking a bath out at the ranch. Not even after the sheep tick incident had he done this. During the night he'd gotten imaginary sensations of ticks in his hair and around his private parts. *That'd be just dandy*, he'd told himself, *the doctor is examining me and a tick comes crawlin' out.*

As instructed, by 0700 Teddy and Tony and a lot of other guys had made the five minute walk from the hotel to the induction station. To some of them it was a lark, more like they were going to summer camp than off to war. A few, who had been drafted, were grim faced but reluctant to openly grouse about it. Teddy, on the other hand, was nervous and scared of what he'd gotten himself into.

Things started out pretty casual. More paperwork, blood pressure check, eye test, hearing test, draw blood, pee in a cup and then it got serious, at least to Teddy it was. A young Navy guy in a white smock gave the order. "Alright, guys, strip."

Another recruit read Teddy's mind. "Everything?"

The sailor parroted back, "Everything."

Teddy took off his clothes, as did the others, and left them in individual piles on the floor behind them.

"Line up and face me," came the command. "The doctor will now examine you. When requested to cough, turn your head to the side before doing so. *Do not* cough in the doctor's face."

The doctor, a middle-aged man with dark hair and rubber gloves, started to Teddy's left at the far end of the line. Teddy couldn't help but watch as each recruit coughed and grimaced while the doctor probed their groins. It was during this process, however, that seeing the others in their nakedness made him feel better about being there. They were by no means all Tonys with hairy chests, moustaches and muscles. Far from it. They reminded him more of his sophomore PE class than men who would soon be put up against fierce Jap soldiers.

And then the doctor was before him. Teddy could smell the coffee on his breath mixed in with his aftershave. "Ever had a hernia?"

"No Sir."

Abruptly, the doctor placed his fingers beneath Teddy's scrotum. "Cough."

Teddy did as he was told.

"Again."

Teddy coughed once more, and the doctor moved on. The process had been more uncomfortable than painful.

The guy next to Teddy, however, was less fortunate. He'd had a hernia in the past. It appeared to Teddy that the doctor was gouging him harder and deeper than the others. The recruit groaned and buckled at the waist and contorted his face in pain. He coughed five times. Teddy counted them. There were tears in the recruit's eyes when the doctor finally relented.

By noon they were all done except for taking the oath. They'd started the morning with about 20 recruits, not all had passed, among them was the guy with the hernia. They were escorted into a room with a podium and the American flag up front. An Army officer was standing behind the podium. He did not give them an option, *maybe a preview of how it's going to be*, thought Teddy. The officer said, "Raise your right hand and repeat after me."

Teddy raised his right hand. "I, Teddy Walker, do solemnly swear that I will support and defend the constitution of the United States against all enemies, foreign and domestic, that I will bear true faith and allegiance to the same; and that I will obey the orders of the President of the United States and the orders of the officers appointed over me according to regulations and the uniform code of military justice, so help me God."

The officer lowered his hand. "Congratulations, men. You're in the military." His words still hung in the air when an Army Sergeant stepped from the side of the room and shouted. "Alright, men, fallout and form up in front of the induction center – ASAP. You've got a train to catch."

In all of his fantasizing about the military, the reality that he would be surrendering his freedom had never hit him like it just did. His mind flashed to the sheep tick incident and how he'd just walked away from that. And then the Sergeant barked again. "Let's get a move on, people."

CHAPTER TWENTY-FIVE

The train pulled into San Diego a few minutes past midnight of the second day. Along the way it had made stops to collect more recruits destined for the Marines and the Navy. By Teddy's estimation there were well over a hundred of them. The smart ones, or maybe the less anxious ones, were asleep when the train came to a stop. A conductor in a black coat and cap with a short bill entered the car and started down the aisle. "San Diego. San Diego,"

A couple of rows up from Teddy and Tony a baby-faced recruit, who hadn't been asleep, asked, "Is this where we get off?"

Although Teddy was certain of the answer, Pete's admonition to *pay attention* sounded in his head. The conductor's expression bordered on pity. "Yes, if San Diego is your destination." And then he moved on wading through recruits that were clogging the aisle.

Teddy nudged Tony and pointed out the window. Two Marines dressed in khaki with wide, flat-brimmed boy scout hats were standing on the platform. "I bet those guys are here for us."

Tony nodded. "We better get out there."

A scared grin came to Teddy's face. "Yeah, I reckon so."

They stood and forced their way into the mob exiting the car. Even before they reached the doorway the shouting from outside could be heard. "C'mon people. Move your sorry asses. I could be home in bed right now if it weren't for you people, and what do you do but lollygag. Fall in, right here."

Teddy stepped from the bright interior of the train car to the duller, shadowy light outside. The night air was warm, much warmer than Montana. He saw where the others were forming ranks and quickened his pace. And then from off to his left the other boy scout hat rushed up to him and shouted within a few feet of his ear. "Are you a cripple? Do you think this is a convention for turtles? Move your bony ass."

The adrenaline surge that hit Teddy's system was painful but effective. He sprinted and took a position in the third rank hoping he would be unnoticed there. Tony fell in beside him. Remembering Pete's advice, Teddy kept his mouth shut. However, another, less intimidated recruit in the front rank laughed nervously and said something to the guy next to him. The Marine with two stripes saw him and immediately pounced. "Who gave you permission to talk?"

The recruit, who was short and skinny with red wavy hair parted on the side, had lots of freckles. He looked into the drill instructor's eyes and was about to speak when the D.I. exploded. "Why are you staring at me, Freckles? What kind of social misfit are you talking out of turn and staring at people? Freckles, your bad manners need correcting. Hit the deck and give me twenty."

Freckles, whose real name was Parry Copeland, dropped to the ground. He'd done three pushups when the D.I. shouted, "count 'em out."

Freckles came back in a loud but shaky voice. "Yes Sir." On the next pushup he shouted, "Four."

The D.I. had been waiting for it, knowing that Freckles would do what most guys would. He mockingly said, "Four, what happened to one, two, three? Start over. I tell ya, it's tough to get good people these days. Are you sure you didn't mean to join the Army?"

Freckles began again. "One pushup, two pushups, three pushups…" When he got to number thirteen his spaghetti arms gave out. He didn't dare look up. His voice was close to breaking. "I can't do anymore."

The D.I. apparently satisfied that he'd made his point said simply, "Get back in line."

There were sixty of them, eyes straight ahead and quiet as mice thanks to Freckles' humiliation. After the rush to fall in they stood there waiting, for what, they didn't know. Teddy had to pee, but he dared not ask to go to the bathroom. He tried telling himself there was a good reason for treating them this way, that if this many young guys were free to talk and grab ass nothing would get done. Finally, a conductor emerged from the train and said something to the DI's. The one with Sergeant's stripes, whose name was Hawkins, turned and walked briskly to the formation of recruits. He stopped directly in front of them and for a few seconds appeared to be evaluating what he had to work with and then he said, "Alright people, there are two buses in front of the depot. I want the first three ranks on the first bus and the second three on the second. Is that clear?"

About half of the recruits, Teddy and Tony among them, shouted, "Yes Sir."

Hawkins frowned at their response and then shouted, "Right, face." Most of the recruits turned to the right. Hawkins followed with simply, "Follow me."

Teddy was glad that he'd met Tony in Bozeman. It gave him some comfort knowing at least one person in all these new faces. They sat together about halfway back on the bus but dared not even whisper to one another. At 0215, after being issued one blanket, they were assigned to a Quonset barracks and allowed to sleep. Teddy had the top bunk, Tony the lower. In the darkness, Teddy stuck his head over the side and whispered, "Whaddaya think so far?"

"Sucks."

From across the way came a curt voice, "Hey Mac, shut the hell up."

Teddy said nothing, knowing that the guy was right. Sleep, however, did not come easy. His mind wandered to his mother and her cell, and in time, the similarities of their confinement. Sometime, much later and not long before reveille, he fell asleep.

CHAPTER TWENTY-SIX

Early on they were made to look like Marines with buzz haircuts and sage green clothing called utilities or dungarees. They were assigned a bunk and taught the Marine way to make a bed. And they were issued a .30 Caliber 1903 Springfield rifle that was not to be confused with a gun. Not being able to recite your rifle's serial number on a moment's notice would get you pushups or some other nefarious punishment. And their stuff, extra clothing, toilet kit and any other personal items the Corps deemed necessary, went into a footlocker at the end of your bunk. There was little about Teddy's daily life that he controlled. Eating, sleeping, going to the head, showering, shaving, even the freedom of talking was all in accordance with the Corps' schedule. Nonetheless, Teddy had surprised himself. He was adapting to Corps life and was glad that he wasn't the guy several bunks over from him that he could hear silently crying in the night. And he was even more proud of not succumbing to deserting like the fat kid from LA who just wanted to go home but got caught in downtown San Diego. Those guys were motivators for Teddy. He allowed himself to think that he was tougher, better than them. It was like they were sacrifices that had to be made to the DI gods. The gods, however, were not easily appeased. Week four of boot camp made that clear to Teddy.

All recruits were required to wash one full set of clothing every day. A bucket, brush and soap had been issued to them for this purpose. A common laundry facility had been constructed near the barracks. Each platoon had its own clothesline and there were faucets sufficient so that each man in the platoon had his own.

Teddy had just completed his washing and was in the process of hanging it to dry when Corporal Miller, one of the assistant DI's, came by. He began scrutinizing Teddy's wash, examining it almost like he would a counterfeit bill. Teddy began to get nervous. He knew better than to speak unless asked to do so. And then it came, his tone of disbelief exaggerated. "What the hell is this?"

Teddy looked over at Miller. He was pointing to a pair of dungarees. A faint, very faint outline of what was once a mud stain could be seen on the left knee. "Is this not a stain?"

Teddy thought about saying he hadn't noticed it but figured that would fly no better than explaining its presence. "Sir, it's from the mud on the obstacle course. I scrubbed it hard, Sir, but it just won't come out, Sir."

"So, you just gave up, huh?"

"Sir, I ran out of time, Sir."

"Bullshit. You were goofing off."

"Sir, no Sir."

"You calling me a liar, Recruit?"

"Sir, no Sir."

"You thought you could just sneak this by? Disgrace the uniform?"

"Sir, no Sir."

Miller suddenly stepped back, shaking his head in disgust. He then looked at the platoon, most of whom were hanging their clothes to dry. He shouted, "Listen up, people. It has come to my attention that you maggots are in need of additional practice in the art of washing clothes. Therefore, you are to remove your clothes from the clothesline and drop them on the ground. When I give the command, you will then march in place on your clothes until I say to stop.

Following this, you will then wash your clothes in the manner in which you've been instructed. Is that clear?"

The platoon shouted, "Sir, yes Sir."

Miller added, "Oh, by the way. Today's lesson is courtesy of Mr. Walker. You be sure and thank him."

Teddy was afraid to look away from his clothes on the line in front of him. He could feel the animosity of the platoon. In that instant, he better understood the fat kid from LA. Teddy reasoned, *if there's a bright spot in this it's that they won't risk getting in trouble for talking to say something snotty to me, at least for a while anyway. On the other hand,* he thought, *they might just give me the cold shoulder when talking is allowed.*

Teddy did not have to wait long for repercussions from the laundry incident. In the evening they usually got an hour of free time to write letters or talk so as to get to know one another. It was as Teddy had envisioned, guys who normally said hi or joked with him, said nothing. Even Tony seemed distant. The pain was real. It left him with a frustrated anger, not at them, but Corporal Miller for inflicting his sick idea of discipline upon them. Teddy's answer was to retreat, not engage any of them, if possible. To that end he was sitting on his footlocker, as opposed to laying on his bed, which was still made to Corps standards, reading his *Guidebook For Marines*. They'd all been issued a copy. It was required reading but not necessarily during free time. *If anything,* thought Teddy, *should Miller walk in he'll be impressed that I'm studying.* But it was not Miller who stopped in front of him. Teddy followed the green clad dungarees up. A big streetwise guy from Seattle named Butch was looking down at him. His shaved head reminded Teddy of a mental patient in a movie that he had seen. "What can I do for you, Butch?"

Butch scowled. "I better not ever have to do my laundry over because of you. If I do, you'll regret it."

Teddy thought for a fleeting second to argue, to apply some common sense to Miller's Marine logic and Butch's need for retribution. In the next instant, however, that common sense came full circle as he gauged the damage that Butch's enormous size could do to him. He said only, "Sorry, Butch."

Butch sneered at him, gloated like he'd just gotten a down payment on what Teddy owed him. He snorted. "Shit bird." And then he walked away.

Teddy watched Butch's departure until he was certain that he wasn't going to circle back and sucker punch him while he was reading. Butch soon melted into a sea of bodies and bunks, but not before he stopped and gave a sideways nod of his head towards Teddy while saying something to a couple of other recruits. They laughed and looked hatefully at Teddy. And then they turned away with one of them patting Butch on the back like he'd just performed a community service. At that moment Teddy wished he was free to just walk out and keep on going right out the front gate. For a few seconds he fantasized doing this. It gave him some relief until the fat kid from LA flashed in his mind followed by Elkhorn. The images caused his inner self to scoff, *where would I go? Damned Pete, if he'd wanted to, he cudda found another job. Some place the both of us could have lived.* Teddy started to shake his head as the picture of his mother and George in the back of the pickup on the way to the hospital came to mind. *Why the hell couldn't she just stay home and tend to business? Damn her. Damn George and damn his worthless bitch of a daughter. Damn 'em all.*

From near the front of the barracks a recruit's voice sounded, "Attention on deck."

Miller's voice came next. "Fall in. Mail call."

The men scrambled to attention, lining each side of the alleyway between the bunks. Teddy looked straight ahead not daring to look at the drill instructor. In a way he hoped there was no mail for him as that would require interaction with Miller.

The ridicule began with Miller laughing while holding up a clutch of letters in his hand. It was like they were a prize he could deny them if he chose to. He reined in his laughter to say, "I'm impressed people. I didn't think any of you knew anybody that could write." He laughed some more, the recruits all stone faced. Before today and the laundry incident, Teddy might have seen it as good-natured teasing, but not now. *What an asshole.* He hoped that his eyes didn't betray him.

Miller called out a name, "Johnson."

A recruit in the line opposite Teddy shouted, "Sir, here Sir," He then stepped forward, paused, executed a left face and trotted to Miller where he extended his hands, as if he were praying, so that Miller could insert the letter between them. Before returning to his place in line he sounded off, "Sir, thank you, Sir."

And so, the routine began with Miller making snide, outrageous comments along the way that caused some laughter for which they didn't get in trouble. It was like he was doing his own comedy skit at the men's expense. On one letter that went to a skinny, pimple faced kid with glasses he made a face like he smelled a skunk. *I didn't know you could put that much cheap perfume on paper.* And on another that was for a tall, studly looking guy, he read off a fictional return address, *Betty's Whorehouse.* This was followed by him holding a letter up and pretending to have trouble reading the name and finally saying, *I don't know, Peterson, it's written in crayon, but I think it's yours.*

Then it came. "Walker."

"Sir, here Sir." Miller was about twenty feet away. Teddy could see it in his face before he got there. He stopped, hopeful Miller would let it pass, but he did not.

Miller held the letter up. He did not laugh as he had the others. Instead, a devious smile came to his face. He read the return address, "Agnes Walker, c/o Elkhorn County Jail, Elkhorn, Montana." Now he laughed. "This a relative of yours?"

Teddy silently cursed his mother for having dropped her married name. But as she explained in a previous letter, she was glad to be rid of Tom Kinney and wanted no part of his name. Teddy, fearful of the consequences to say otherwise, told Miller what he wanted to hear. "Sir, yes Sir."

For whatever reason, Miller knowingly pushed on past the boundary of humor. "This your sister? She a street-walker?" A few of the crass amongst the men laughed, likely seeking favor with Miller.

Teddy, still standing with his hands prayerfully extended, came back, "Sir, no Sir. Agnes is my mother Sir. She is in jail for killing my stepfather, Sir."

No one laughed. Not even the sycophants. If Miller was embarrassed he didn't show it, as he inserted the letter between Teddy's hands. He moved on shouting out another name, "Perkins." But that's all he said. There were no more jokes. Soon, he was gone.

Teddy climbed into his bunk avoiding eye contact with Tony who was in the lower one. He figured it would be awkward between them now on account of he had lied to Tony about his mother. He laid down staring at the ceiling. Before today, he'd told himself the Marines were ok, that he could cut it. Now, he wasn't sure. He looked at Agnes' letter, the same one that Miller had just humiliated him with. He wished there would be something good in it, something that would cheer him up, but he knew better. He sighed and opened it.

My Dearest Teddy,

I was glad to hear that the Marines agrees with you. Maybe they can give you the home that I never could. I am proud of you. Pete came to see me today. It was the first time since that day you and him came by on your way to enlist. His coming wasn't his own idea, however. My lawyer, the public defender, drove out to the ranch to see if he and George would be character witnesses at my sentencing next week. Pete agreed but George did not. I misjudged those two but in different ways. George is a scalawag of the highest order. Pete, on the other hand, is no choir boy, but I obviously rate him higher than George. You should know too that I am certain Pete is your father. He agreed with me on that matter when he was here today. He even said that when I get out of prison we could "get together". I'm not holding my breath on that happening, but it might be ok if it did. What do you think? You could come live with your jailbird parents! (Ha, Ha)

My lawyer says the least amount of time that I'll get is two years. That doesn't seem right to me as I truly believe Tom would have killed George had I not shot him. Maybe I should have called out to him or fired a warning shot, but the truth is I was afraid of him. When I stepped into that room and saw how he was beating George all I could think was, I've got to stop him. Another lesson in life, I guess.

I think it is nice that you write to Pete. He told me today that he looks forward to getting your letters and is going to write you one back tonight. I will write you next week and let you know how my day in court goes. Oh my, look at the mail you will be getting! Be safe.

Your Loving Mother

Teddy read the letter a second time before folding it and putting it back in the envelope. For a time, he laid there with his hands and the letter resting on his chest. He stared up at the rivets that held the sections of the Quonset hut in place. His mind's eye began to fantasize the life that Agnes had suggested. He tuned out the din of the recruits measured freedom allowing his fantasy to grow. He and Pete would get jobs on a big ranch. There'd be a house for them to live in, a real house, not a shack. And Agnes would take care of the house and tend her garden and cook for them and once a week they'd go to town for burgers and a picture show. A happy feeling was welling up inside Teddy when the lights went off and then on. Miller shouted, "Five minutes, lights out."

Teddy hopped down from his bunk and began getting ready for bed. From the corner of his eye, he saw that Tony was already under his blankets. He was looking up at him. Teddy whispered, "I'm sorry."

Tony whispered back, "I would've done the same thing."

It was a relief to Teddy that Tony had not pitched his tent in Butch's camp. He knew there would be those that would hold the laundry thing against him. He reckoned he could deal with them, but not Tony too.

CHAPTER TWENTY-SEVEN

In spite of the laundry and letter incidents, Teddy felt better about himself and his future. Agnes' letter gave him hope that they would be a family one day. With their past, he recognized that they would never be candidates for a Norman Rockwell painting on the cover of the Saturday Evening Post. He would settle for just living in a decent house, even if they didn't own it, and breaking bread together without it degenerating into a yelling match. After a week of visualizing the place they would have, it had become stuck in his mind. It was a nice white house with green trim and a brick chimney. And there was a lawn surrounded by a cedar board fence that was freshly stained. Big ponderosa pine trees shadowed the whole thing and beyond them was his mother's garden. It was bucolic, his go-to place that allowed him to become almost immune from Miller's rants or the pain of long runs or calisthenics or snapping in his rifle for the thousandth time. Before the letter, he wondered if his mother had the same life dream as he did. Now, he no longer wondered.

They were on the rifle range when Teddy saw a jeep with two officers in it drive up and stop. He watched as Miller immediately double-timed over to them and saluted. The officers' faces were serious. Very soon, Miller's was too. He turned and pointed towards Teddy. The officer in the passenger seat looked and nodded. Adrenaline laced fear suddenly seized Teddy's insides. His face was hot. The shooting behind him became distant, unable to compete with the pounding of his heart within his ears. And then Miller started towards Teddy. They'd had eye contact since the jeep. The old Miller, the usually abrasive Miller, would have screamed for Teddy to come to him. Today, this person that Teddy didn't recognize walked to within a few feet of him. His voice was calm. "Walker, you need to go with those guys in the jeep."

Teddy knew better. Fear kicked the words out. "Sir, what's this about, Sir?"

Miller did not lash out at him for questioning the order. His serious face had become almost sad. "They'll tell you."

Teddy's inner voice, the one that seldom had anything good to say, shouted, *They found out how old you are. They're gonna boot you out.* Teddy kept on like a condemned man going to the gallows. His executioners sat grim faced in the jeep. When he was nearly there, the one in the passenger seat, a Major, climbed in the back. Teddy recognized him from the Sunday service that most all of them attended. The captain behind the wheel, who was Teddy's company commander, gestured toward the empty seat. "Hop in."

Teddy sat down in the space vacated by the major. At first they just sat there, Teddy staring straight ahead through the jeep's windshield at another rifle range beyond them. The crack of the Springfield rifles, often many at once, reminded Teddy of a string of firecrackers going off on the fourth of July. And then the captain put his hand on Teddy's shoulder. "Son, I've got some bad news for you."

Teddy looked at him.

"Your folks have been killed."

Teddy instantly felt as if he could throw up. He forgot about Marine speak and stammered, "Wha-what? How did this happen?"

The captain, his hand still on Teddy's shoulder, came back, "Your mother had a court proceeding?"

Teddy nodded. "She wrote me about it."

"Apparently your stepfather's sister was one of those that gave testimony. According to what your recruiter read in the paper things went ok until the judge issued his decision. And then this woman pulled a pistol from her purse and shot your mother and the judge. According to the paper she would have killed the prosecutor if it hadn't been for your father jumping in to try and disarm her. Unfortunately, he was killed before a deputy killed this woman. I'm sorry."

Teddy closed his eyes, trying to hold the tears back. His inner voice, bitter and hateful, shouted it out, *I was within two years of being normal, of being happy. Just too damned much to ask for, I guess.*

From behind Teddy, the chaplain said, "Your folks have already been buried but I can still arrange for emergency leave so you can go home."

Teddy snorted, ignoring the fact he was talking to a Marine Major. "Home, I ain't got any home but right here."

"You've got no family back there?"

Teddy shook his head just as a particularly intense salvo of firing erupted off to his right.

"Would you like to talk? We could go back to the chapel where it's quiet."

Teddy snuffled. "Sir, I don't know what there is to say that would make any of this better."

"Perhaps we could pray?"

Teddy knew he shouldn't say it, but he did anyway. "Sir, I figure if God wanted to help me, he would've been in that courtroom and stopped that woman from killing my folks, Sir."

It became quiet again save for the rifle fire, while the chaplain considered God's response. Teddy averted his eyes to the speedometer lest he make contact with either of them. The speedometer went to sixty, its white needle now laying over to zero. There were 12,316.4 miles on the jeep. And then the chaplain said, "God's ways are not always easy to understand. Just remember, in the end, he has your best interest at heart."

The naysayer in Teddy's mind laughed sarcastically and shouted, *that's a bunch of crap*. In good Marine speak, he said aloud, "Sir, I believe God may have off days when he forgets about some of us, Sir."

"Do you mind if we pray, Teddy?"

The inner Teddy escaped. "Sir, I reckon the cow is already outta the barn, Sir."

"I'll say a prayer for you, Teddy. Remember though, you can come talk to me any time."

Teddy nodded as the captain chimed in, "Why don't you take the afternoon off, maybe go to the PX or the USO? I'll write you a pass."

Teddy pondered the offer. *Ma and Pete are dead. It won't matter where I go or what I do they'll still be dead.* He said aloud, "Sir, I believe I'd just as soon stay here with my platoon."

The captain glanced at the chaplain before coming back to Teddy. "Alright, suit yourself."

Teddy got out of the jeep, saluted and started back to his place on the firing line. He was not quite out of earshot when he heard the chaplain say, "He's a cold one, that boy is."

CHAPTER TWENTY-EIGHT

The 17th of May, Teddy's birthday, came and went with no one knowing except him. On that day he thought how it would have been if his mother and Pete hadn't been killed. She'd have written a happy birthday letter and Pete might have written a second letter. His first arrived the day after Teddy got word that he was dead. It would have been enough of a present had it turned out that way. Instead, he got pity which was ok too. It had begun the day he found out. He wasn't sure if it was God answering the chaplain's prayer, or Miller and most of the platoon finding a streak of compassion on their own. Butch and a few of his cronies being the exception. Regardless, that day had come and gone and the one they had all been waiting for had arrived. They'd risen extra early to make sure their uniforms and weapons were immaculate. They'd rehearsed how and where they'd march. Butterflies amongst them were rampant as were head calls just before they fell in outside their barracks. And then they marched to the band's music passing in review of the *big shots,* as Tony called them, and family and friends. Neither Teddy nor Tony had anyone in the stands for them. With Montana being as far away as it was and Teddy's situation more obvious, nobody came. And they stood, not so patiently, listening to one of the big shots tell them what good Marines they were and the sacrifice they were making for their country. Finally, it was over. The prize the Corps had dangled in front of them for eight long weeks was now theirs. They were Marines. More importantly to Teddy, the Corps had given him something nobody could ever take away, pride. He was no longer Walker trash, at least for now he wasn't.

Early the next morning they were on a bus going up the coast to Camp Pendleton. Almost all their companions for the past two months were on those buses as well. Corporal Miller, however, was not. In a few days he would start the re-shaping of the minds and bodies of sixty new recruits. Teddy vacillated in his regret for not seeking Miller out at gradua-tion and thanking him for treating him like a human being after the deaths of his parents. At one point they'd made eye contact in the milling crowd of recruits and civilians. He'd started towards Miller, having mostly convinced himself that Miller had been justified in turning the platoon against him. And then, who should step up and shake Miller's hand but Butch. Their smiles were mutual. In his mind, Teddy could still hear Miller, *Good luck Butch*. Even now, Teddy's inner voice screamed at him. *Are you kidding me? Butch? Good luck, Butch. The biggest asshole in the platoon and he calls him by his first name and pats him on the back.*

Teddy was grateful, however, for Tony. They had been assigned to the same company of infantrymen. They bunked next to one another. Tony was the big brother Teddy never had. In the three weeks they'd been at Camp Pendleton they'd learned a lot about one another. Teddy knew that Tony's parents were ranchers and that they'd never been in trouble with the law and that he had a younger brother and older sister and a girlfriend. And he knew that he got lots of mail. Teddy on the other hand, got nothing, a fact that was common knowledge to most everyone in the company.

Today was another rehearsal of what was coming. At least in part it was. The Higgins boats had tied up next to a pier that extended a longways out into the ocean. It was a blustery, overcast morning. A stiff easterly wind had a windsock on shore standing straight out. Had the men of G Company been wearing anything other than helmets, they would have been blown off. Even tethered as they were, the boats rocked and banged occasionally against the big water smoothed pilings that smelled of the ocean. Gulls overhead complained as they labored to stay on course. As they neared their boat, Teddy looked out at the frothy lines of white endlessly rolling towards the beach. "I sure hope we don't go out very far. I enjoyed my breakfast too much to heave it over the side."

Tony laughed. "Now what'd Harper say? *You can't always go to war on a bluebird day.*"

Teddy was about to respond when Sergeant Harper came up behind them. He shouted above the wind and idling engines of the boats. "If you two knuckleheads are done gabbing, would you mind getting in the boat?"

It was about two feet down to the lip that ran along the upper edges of the boat. Teddy gripped his rifle with his right hand and held his helmet on with his left as he jumped. From there he hopped into the interior of the already crowded boat. They were shoulder to shoulder, like cattle stuffed in a train car. It was Tony who voiced the fear in their minds. "I sure as hell hope this thing stays afloat."

The Navy coxswain, standing at the controls, remained grim faced saying nothing to ease the tension. Teddy hoped the sailor wasn't as scared as he was. Finally, they cast off and headed out to the open water. As far as he could see, the waves were swelling white and angry. The boat pitched like a carnival roller coaster. The big shots had told Harper, who'd told the Navy guy, to take it out about a mile and then circle until all the boats were there. *Got to be just like the real thing,* he'd said. *Get online. Assault the beach together.*

The puking began before they were halfway to where they would circle. Teddy was among the sick. He'd purposely stood next to the edge of the boat so he could send his breakfast over the side. Others trapped in the mass of bodies incurred the wrath of their fellow Marines. Teddy, on the other hand, had learned his lesson with the laundry.

On they went climbing up wave after wave only to crash down into a trough and a shower of water. The smell of vomit became infectious precipitating even more sickness. At last, they reached the arbitrary assembly point. It had now begun to rain. Teddy had puked two more times. He looked to shore. The pier was a tiny speck. The naysayer in his mind lashed out. *This is bullshit. Everybody in this damned boat will be so damned sick by the time we get to the beach we'll be lucky to just stand up.* And then Teddy's boat, one of the first there, began to circle. It was only then that he recognized they would be there a while before the other boats reached them. He nudged Tony and pointed to the boats in the distance. Tony frowned and shook his head. Had Sergeant Harper not been nearby Teddy would have groused out loud.

The rain had intensified to the point that Teddy reasoned, *anybody with a lick of sense would put an end to this.* It was beyond forever, and about the time the lightning began, that one of the big shots gave the order to begin the landing. Teddy's nausea and dizziness was unrelenting. He regretted ever joining the Marines. He tried not to, to blame the dead, but the naysayer in his mind took over and leveled charges against Pete and Agnes. *If she hadn't been sleeping around, I wouldn't be here. Or, if Pete would've just manned up and found another job and taken me in, I'd be in history class about now.*

And then a young baby-faced Lieutenant standing next to Harper shouted, "Men, prepare to land. When the gate drops advance inland. Take up positions on the bunkers. We'll practice fire and maneuver tactics to take them out."

The wind and rain and splash of the waves were incessant. By the time the boats dropped their gates on the beach the men were soaked and chilled to their core. Some to the point their teeth were chattering. Teddy's stomach hurt from having retched so hard. His squad leader, a Corporal Wilkens from Alabama, had told them to give a rebel yell when they hit the beach. *Put the fear of God and the Corps in them*, he'd said. However, the effects of the ocean stifled most of them. Teddy staggered under the weight of his wet pack and the effects of the seasickness until they reached another seemingly arbitrary place and Wilkens ordered, "take cover." Teddy collapsed into the wet sand. He savored its stability, so glad to be out of the damned boat. Straight out from him, maybe a hundred yards away, was a machine gun emplacement made of logs and sandbags. A horizontal slot about six inches high by three feet wide allowed the gun inside to spew bullets over a wide area. Today it was firing blanks as was Teddy and the others. His squad would lay down a base fire that, in theory, would allow the squad to their right to assault the gun and destroy it.

Wilkens yelled, "Commence firing."

Teddy worked the bolt on his Springfield rifle and took aim at the middle of the skinny window. He pulled the trigger causing his rifle to roar and buck up. A cacophony of gunfire erupted. Men to either side of him were furiously working their bolts. Hot brass occasionally flipped out onto Teddy. He fired his five rounds, reloaded and had nearly exhausted that when a big shot blew a whistle followed by shouts of "cease fire." The big shots and Wilkens declared them victorious. Teddy, on the other hand, wondered if it had been the Japs in that pillbox if he wouldn't be dead. His cover had been a shelf of hard packed sand less than a foot high. Too much of him had been visible to survive. A conference of the big shots had convened in front of the gun emplacement, no doubt to plan a second iteration. This time Teddy's squad would be the ones assaulting the gun. Teddy took advantage of the lull, not even raising up from his firing position. He lay there, listening to his ears ring from the gunfire. They'd started in boot camp and never stopped. He'd asked Wilkens to go on sick call about it. He just laughed, *join the club*. And then he laughed some more.

They continued to run the exercise alternating roles, pausing long enough at noon to eat c rations in the wind and rain. By 1500 the big shots decreed that it was time to go back to the barracks. But there would be no trucks. They were going to *hump it*, five miles in the rain. Two miles into the march, Teddy, who'd not eaten all of his cold canned chicken and dry biscuit declared to Tony, "I don't care what they got for supper, I'm lickin' my tray clean."

Tony came back, his head down, rain dripping off his helmet, "I may be too damned tired to eat."

"Ah, c'mon, don't crap out on me. I was hoping to go to the USO tonight. I'll buy ya a Coke."

Tony snickered. "I know why you want to go over there and it ain't for a coke."

"You'd go to if you didn't already have a girl."

Tony laughed. "Yeah, there's a couple of those dollies workin' there that'll make a fella's eyes tired lookin' at'em."

Teddy caught Tony's attention. "Just one Coke?"

Out of nowhere, Wilkens came at a brisk pace along side of them and shouted, "Do I need to put a boot in y'all's ass?"

In unison, they said quickly, "No Sir." And picked up the pace.

When Wilkens had gotten sufficiently ahead of them, Tony whispered, "Just one."

CHAPTER TWENTY-NINE

It came as no surprise to Teddy that his plans for the evening did not mesh with what Sergeant Harper had in mind. They'd stowed their gear, showered and changed clothes before chow thinking that afterwards they would have some free time to go to the USO.

Nobody's going anywhere, Harper had shouted, *until your rifles are cleaned and these floors are mopped.*

They had complied, some more diligently than others. By 2030 the barracks met with Harper's approval, but not without his admonition of what this would mean. *Any of you clowns taking a stroll to the PX or the USO tonight, just remember lights out at 2200.*

Here and there were puddles of water in the street. The rain had slackened to a light mist. It was hardly bothersome as in places the clouds had given way to the stars.

"The things I don't do for you, Walker."

Teddy laughed. "Hey, you're gettin' a free Coke."

"Do I need to ask this girl out for you?"

"Her name's Olivia and no, I'll do it."

"When?"

"I don't know. I just learned her name a couple of days ago."

"You shudda asked her then."

"Easy for you to say."

"You ever been on a date?"

It suddenly got quiet save for the scuffling of their boots on the pavement.

Tony came back. "You haven't, have you?"

Teddy glanced over his shoulder lest he confess within earshot of one of the womanizers in the barracks. His voice was barely above a whisper. "No, not really."

"What's not really?"

"I've danced with girls after ball games."

"So, you've never kissed a girl?"

Teddy hesitated, looking at the reflections of the street lights in the puddles. Every now and again a drop of rain would land in one of the puddles. For a few seconds, concentric circles would appear marking the drop's entry point and then they were gone. Teddy's thoughts went back to Elkhorn and that day on the lunch bus. He wished that he was a Mormon and Becky would have gone out with him and they would have kissed and he would get letters from her at mail call. At last, he said, "No, I ain't never kissed a girl."

Another awkward pause sprung up between them. Teddy's angst grew in anticipation of how it would be resolved. The answer came in a considerate whisper, "So, how old are you, really?"

Teddy took a breath, mostly to steady his voice. "You can't tell anybody."

"I know."

"I just turned sixteen."

"Sixteen. How'd you get in?"

It briefly crossed Teddy's mind to be truthful, to tell how Pete blackmailed the recruiter. But he knew there were some things that it was best if they were never told, not even to a friend. He said only, "My dad lied about my age."

"He'd do that for you?"

Teddy thought to tell how it was with him and Pete before he put out what had loaded itself on his tongue. "It's what I wanted."

Tony snorted. "For me, I was about to get drafted. And one day I just decided I'd rather be in the Marines than the Army. To tell you the truth though, I ain't sure why I'm here because just between you, me and the fence post, I ain't all gung ho to go kill Japs."

A surprised look came to Teddy's face. He looked over at Tony. "Me neither."

"I guess it'll be our secret."

Teddy nodded. "It will, but you've got more secrets on me than I do you."

Tony grinned. "They're all safe."

By and by they came to a large, green wooden building that housed the USO. It had lots of well-lit windows. Through them Teddy could see the snack bar where Olivia worked. It was about three deep in Marines waiting for a milkshake or soft drink.

They stepped inside. The cigarette smoke was, as the saying goes, thick enough to cut with a knife. A jukebox along the left wall was playing a Tommy Dorsey song, its volume running a distant second to the din of pool balls clacking, loud talk, laughter and the tinny whine of the milk shake machine. Six pool tables, one after another, sat crosswise in the long rectangular room. To either side of them were tables and chairs and racks of cue sticks on the walls. A light shade suspended from the ceiling hung over each pool table.

Near the door, but a long way from the snack bar, was an empty table. They sat down. Tony lit a Camel, took a drag and then made his contribution to the blue haze in the room. He laughed. "Looks like you got plenty of competition."

Teddy frowned. "You ready for your Coke?"

"Sure."

Teddy stood up. "I'll be back in a minute."

A wry grin came over Tony's face. "They got a coupla waitresses here, ya know."

For a few seconds Teddy was suckered in, then he came back, "Smartass."

The crowd at the snack bar had thinned out but not to the point Teddy could walk up and order. *It's just as well*, he thought, *I don't know what to say*. His heart was hammering. He looked at the other Marines comparing himself to them. *They've probably all been with girls and know what to do.* And then he allowed his eyes to settle on Olivia, not quite a stare but close. She was scooping ice cream and dropping the scoops into a tall metal container. If she had seen him she didn't let on. Her long black hair and dark eyes contrasted with her white blouse. She was buxom. With the exception of a glimpse he'd accidentally gotten of Agnes changing her clothes one time, he had no personal knowledge of such things. Her laugh came easy. *She's probably got a good life*, thought Teddy. *She probably won't want me in it. Another Becky.* And then it was like she'd known all along he'd been watching her. She looked at him and smiled weakly. Her eyes had become uncomfortable as she picked up the metal container with the scoops of ice cream and turned to the back counter. The green blender struggled against the frozen ice cream surging ahead one moment and in the next falling back. A bad feeling was coming over Teddy that suddenly justified itself. Butch appeared at the far end of the counter, but he did not stop there. He came right around it and walked up to Olivia. Her laugh returned. "What are you doing?"

He looked down at her. "Just came by to make sure we're still on for tomorrow night. Dinner and dancing."

Her happy smile had come back. "Yes, I'll pick you up at the main gate at seven."

Teddy's inner voice shouted. *She's picking him up.*

Butch grinned. "That's 1900 to a Marine."

Olivia gave a playful salute. "Yes Sir."

And then knowing damn good and well that he had an envious audience, Butch placed his meaty right hand in the small of Olivia's back and pulled her slightly to him. He kissed her on the lips. Teddy was certain she'd be repulsed by it. Instead, she briefly feigned shock before laughing. "You better get out of here while I still have a job."

Butch looked across the counter flashing what Teddy thought looked like a victory smile. He roved his eyes over the men, gloating until he came to Teddy, whereupon he paused and drew up a mocking smile making sure that Teddy saw that it was just for him.

Teddy couldn't help but glare at Butch. *What an asshole. What does she see in him*? He shook his head and walked away hoping that Olivia saw he'd left without his drinks.

"So, where's my Coke?"

Teddy sat down. "Like you said, they got a coupla waitresses here."

A blend of sadness and anger was plastered on Teddy's face. Tony came back. "Didn't go well?"

"She's going out tomorrow night with Butch."

"You're kidding."

"Why would a girl like her go out with a guy like him?"

Tony sighed. "Maybe she doesn't know the real Butch?"

"How couldn't she? You hear the way he talks in the barracks. Sounds like he's been with lots of women and he ain't too particular."

Tony laughed. "I'm surprised he hasn't caught one of those social diseases they told us about in boot camp."

"Serve him right if he did and his tallywhacker rotted off."

Tony laughed again as he motioned for the waitress. He said, about the time she got to the table, "There's lots a fish in the sea, Teddy."

She said, "You boys drinkin' or fishin'?"

"Drinkin'." Said Teddy, "two Cokes."

CHAPTER THIRTY

It was about two weeks after the night at the USO that they rode buses down to San Diego and got on several big Navy ships, the kind that would take them to the islands where the Japs were waiting for them. They would be at sea for several days, they'd been told. This was a final rehearsal. There were thousands of men on the ships, just like it would be when they did it for real. Quarters were tight. Secrets were non-existent. So, it had been the night before when Teddy had overheard Butch and another guy. The pertinent parts, the parts that even now Teddy found painful went something like this.

Butch, you still sleepin' with that USO babe?

You better believe it. She's wild in the sack.

I don't see what she sees in you.

Butch laughs. *Me neither.* He laughs again.

Today was their last day. One more time of climbing down the cargo nets to where they could drop the final three feet to the Higgins boat. The order had been given to go over the side. Teddy's platoon was next. He and Tony were working their way forward to where they would start down the net.

Tony, who fared no better than Teddy with seasickness, said in a low voice, "I'm ready to be on some solid ground."

Teddy came back, perhaps cocky beyond his abilities, "Me too, even if I got to fight a Jap for it. Just let me off this damned boat."

From behind him came Butch's unmistakable sarcasm. "That I gotta see. A candy-ass like you."

Teddy turned and gave Butch a dirty look. His tongue then got away from him, "Stuff it, asshole."

Butch seethed the words as he stepped towards Teddy, "Why you little prick."

And then another guy, a private just like them but as big as Butch, said in a sour voice, "Why don't you two idiots save it for the Japs?"

Butch scowled at the intruder and then to Teddy, "I ain't gonna let this slide, dipshit. Your time's comin'."

Teddy said nothing. No threatening look. Just turned his back to Butch lest he see the fear surface in his momentary bravado.

At the rail, Sergeant Harper called out, "Choppy water today, men. So, pay attention to what you're doing."

Teddy looked out to the sea. There were whitecaps, not real high but too high for his comfort. They'd practiced debarkation on shore climbing down cargo nets suspended from a wooden wall, but this was different. He was seasick and felt trembly weak. And he was afraid. The naysayer in his mind shouted at him, *you're a snot-nosed kid in a man's world.* Then he was there, at the edge. A mumbled whisper escaped him. "Shit, that's a longways down."

Harper stepped close. "Grip the cable railing tight. Get a firm toe hold in the net and then go on down. You'll be ok."

Teddy glanced over at Harper. He thought he saw a hint of fatherly kindness in his eyes until suddenly he came back, "C'mon Walker, get a move on."

To his right, Tony had just climbed over the top cable like it was a barbed wire fence back home. He was firmly on the net and starting down when he looked up at Teddy. "Nuthin' to it." He laughed. "I'll catch you if you fall."

Teddy gathered his courage. "Alright, I'm coming your way." He applied a white-knuckle grip to the cable while probing the net with first his right foot and then the left. He made certain that his feet were secure in the loops before letting go of the cable and gripping the top part of the net. The immediate sensation that his heavy pack and rifle would pull him away caused his heart to catapult into his throat.

Tony called up. "You good."

Teddy forced himself to say, "Yeah, coming down." He'd negotiated in a slow and deliberate fashion four rows of the rope squares when up above he heard Butch. "C'mon Walker, you chickenshit. The war's gonna be over before you even get in the boat."

Teddy thought to tell Butch, *go screw yourself*, when Harper barked, "Shut your mouth, private." Seconds later he followed up. "You think this is so damned easy show us how it's done."

Butch frowned in a smug way and stepped around the guy in front of him and climbed over the cable. He did not hesitate to start down the net. His intent no doubt was to pass Teddy, to embarrass him. Within seconds he succeeded in getting to where Teddy was on the net, still a longways up. He'd bounded there almost like a logger with climbing spikes belted to a tree, except he had neither. He sneered at Teddy. "Pussy." And then it happened. Butch's right foot slipped out of the next loop. His arms immediately straightened under his weight and the pack and rifle. His feet began to frantically bicycle in thin air desperate to snag a loop. For a few seconds, Teddy thought Butch might succeed. But then he fell away backwards, the terror in his eyes permanently fixed in Teddy's mind. As luck, or perhaps in Butch's case, Karma, would have it, the Higgins boat rocked away from the ship just far enough that the back of his head smacked the edge of it. His body then went limp as a rag doll and collapsed into the roiling abyss between the two boats. Shouts of, "Man overboard" rang out above and below Teddy. Soon, very soon, a sailor with a life preserver appeared at the top of the net. But he did not toss it down as the same forces that had saw fit for the Higgins boat to dance away from the ship now brought it back. Somewhere beneath it, probably on his way to the bottom of the sea, was Butch.

CHAPTER THIRTY-ONE

The cooks had held chow for them. They were late in finishing the training exercise. First they had to be sure that Butch was dead, that he hadn't surfaced somewhere and was endlessly treading water. And then, they had to take statements while it was still fresh in the minds of those who witnessed what had happened. Teddy avoided saying that Butch died being reckless in trying to upstage him. On the other hand, Sergeant Harper did not hold back. Teddy was glad, even though he feared criticizing the dead.

Butch was with Teddy throughout the night falling over and over. At some point, he began calling to Teddy for help. Later on, towards dawn, the old Butch appeared threatening Teddy for letting him die. And so it was on this morning Teddy welcomed the sound of reveille.

They were standing in formation outside taking roll prior to going on a three mile run when a green sedan pulled up. A lieutenant that Teddy didn't recognize got out and went straight to Harper like he had serious business. They talked in low voices for less than a minute whereupon Harper turned and looked at Teddy. "Private Walker, go with the Lieutenant."

Like a trained seal, Teddy barked back, "Yes, Sergeant." Everybody's eyes were upon him as he worked his way from the interior of the formation. They knew as well as Teddy that a strange officer coming for you probably wasn't a good thing. The stranger, who was wearing utilities just like Teddy, started for the car almost before Teddy reached him. Over his shoulder, he said, "Get in the back, Private."

"Yes Sir." A fearful feeling descended upon Teddy as he opened the passenger side rear door. He got in and closed the door. It was an older car. The smell of cigarettes was strong, almost overwhelming to a non-smoker. His mind began to work. *This is like being hauled off by the cops. Gotta be about Butch. Already told 'em my side of that.*

The Lieutenant had just shifted into second gear when his eyes appeared in the rearview mirror. They were green and non-threatening. "You like the Marines, Private?"

"Yes Sir."

The eyes didn't change. They just sprang it on Teddy. "What year were you born?"

In the past, most everyone had asked straight out, how old are you? Not that it mattered, he fumbled. "Nineteen twenty-.uh, four, Sir."

The eyes smiled. "They got the goods on you, Private."

"Goods, Sir?"

"Somebody back in your hometown ratted you out to the recruiter there."

In that instant Teddy could think of no one who would do such a thing. "Who, Sir? Who was it?"

"That's confidential."

"Sir, I got no place to go but the Corps. Seems like it's only fair that I know who wants to take that away."

The eyes looked back to the street as the car slowed and turned right.

Teddy looked into the mirror. "Please, Sir."

"You need to ask the colonel that."

"Sir, you know he won't tell me."

"And if I do and you blab to someone that I did, it'll be my ass."

"Sir, I promise, I won't tell a soul."

The Lieutenant frowned and shook his head. And then he just spit it out, curt and regretful. "Gladys Wilson, you know her?"

Teddy's immediate reaction was, *who in the hell is Gladys Wilson?* He grappled with the name while the Lieutenant waited for his response. And then the mystery solved itself as Pete's letter sounded in his mind. *...your ma has gotten pretty chummy with this Gladys Wilson that brings her meals. That's all fine and well but she told the woman about you joining the Corps. So, this busy body says to me, kind of snotty like, what a shame it is that my boy has to quit school and join the Marines. Made me feel like a turd for a while but she don't know how things are for us.* Teddy came back, "No Sir. Never heard of her."

The Lieutenant gave Teddy a vacant look as he likely didn't know anything about Gladys other than her name. Shortly, they pulled to the curb in front of yet another green wooden building. It was two stories, full of offices and big shots. A reddish sign with yellow lettering that was planted in the grass to the right of the door said it was the Battalion Headquarters. Teddy followed the Lieutenant inside. They removed their caps and started down a long hallway with open office doors to either side. Teddy noted the dark wood floor. *Mopped and waxed by some private*, he thought. And then they came to the very end of the hall and stepped into an outer office where a corporal with wire rim glasses was sitting behind a gray metal desk. His look, and the fact he immediately started for the Colonel's door, told Teddy that he already knew what was going on. "I'll tell the Colonel you're here." He went inside, not quite latching the door. Their voices were surprisingly muffled compared to the Marines Teddy was used to being around. The Corporal reappeared. "You can go in now."

They went through the door with the Corporal closing it behind them. Before either of them could speak the

Colonel looked at Teddy. "So, you're the eager beaver from Montana?"

Teddy came back quick, hoping to make a good impression. "Yes Sir."

The Colonel curled a paper up from where it was laying on his desk to where he could read it, as if he hadn't read it plenty of times before now. "Says here you're from Elkhorn."

"Yes Sir."

"I'm from Livingston."

Teddy became hopeful. "Sir, my best buddy in the platoon is from Livingston."

"Small world. What's his name?"

"Halverson, Sir. Tony Halverson."

"Well, I'll be go to hell. My folks' place was just down the road from theirs. Frank and Doris King."

"I'll tell him, Sir. He'd probably like to know that so he could pass it on to his folks."

Yeah, do that. I betcha I know his dad, Luke. Is his name Luke?"

"Don't know, Sir, but I can find out."

"Yeah, do that. Pass it on to your Sergeant. Tell him I want to know."

"Yes Sir, I'll do that."

And then the good ole boy in the Colonel's face went away. He sighed. "I guess you know you've got yourself in a real jackpot here."

"Sir, I didn't have much of a choice."

"The Corps frowns on liars, you know that don't you?"

"Yes Sir, I just didn't have any place to go."

The Colonel nodded. "I know some of your situation and I'm sorry for your loss but there are rules, hard rules."

Teddy's eyes got watery. "Sir, I've got nowhere to go. The Corps is my home."

The Colonel noted how Teddy was. It caused him to sigh again, even more deeply, and look away. He picked up a pack of Chesterfield cigarettes from his desk, shook one out and lit it. He drew on it and blew the smoke to his side. Quiet enveloped the office. In the distance they could hear the sing-song cadence of running Marines. It was second only to the ringing in Teddy's ears. The Colonel took a second drag studying Teddy as he did. When the last of the smoke had left his mouth he said, "You know I'm supposed to put you on a bus for home."

Teddy said nothing, resigned pretty much to what was coming.

"But I guess that's what complicates this whole thing, you don't have a home to go to."

"No Sir, I don't."

It was clear to Teddy the Colonel was frustrated, apprehensive of what he was about to do, finally he said, "Private Walker, here's the way I see things. The Corps has spent time and money training you to be an infantryman. But, since you're only sixteen years old there would likely be some ladies sewing circle that would pitch a fit if you was denied the opportunity to live one more year of life before getting yourself killed by the Japs. So here's the deal, you can finish your training as a rifleman but when it comes time to ship out you'll be reassigned to a quartermaster company, most likely kitchen police right here on post. How does that suit you?"

Teddy knew better than to argue. He knew too that if the Colonel hadn't been from Livingston, he'd probably be on a bus this afternoon. He said simply, "Thank you, Sir."

The Colonel nodded looking Teddy hard in the eyes. "Keep this to yourself. You got me out on a limb here, so don't saw it off."

"Yes Sir."

"That'll be all."

It wasn't until Teddy and the Lieutenant were out in the hall that he allowed himself a cautious grin. *Now,* he thought, *if Gladys Wilson will just mind her own business.*

CHAPTER THIRTY-TWO

For a time, the barracks scuttlebutt was Butch had got himself killed because he was so pissed at Teddy. A few people blamed Teddy for being slow on the nets while others blamed Harper for ordering Butch over the side when he was agitated. However, the people who mattered, the big shots, put the blame on Butch and his reckless temper. His behavior on that day he was to become fish food was served up as a warning on every debarkation exercise thereafter. By the end of the summer it was unnecessary, especially to those men who had heard Butch yell on his way down and then the '*thunk*' of his head hitting the Higgins boat and finally the splash without a peep from an apparently unconscious Butch.

The Rusty Bucket was just off post. It had become Teddy and Tony's favorite place to go for a couple of reasons. One, it didn't card Marines, not even baby-faced ones like Teddy. And two, it had a pretty waitress that had taken a liking to Teddy.

It was a hot summer evening. The sun appeared to be floating on the ocean a long way out. They'd worked up a sweat hiking to *The Bucket* as they called it. Wet stains crept out from their armpits. A neon sign advertising *Cold Beer* next to the image of a foamy mug hung in the flyspecked window next to the door. They stepped inside to the smokey drunken chatter.

Tony pointed to the back of the room, beyond the dance floor surrounded by tables and chairs. "There's Maria."

Teddy looked over just as a Marine with a beer in one hand put his other hand on her shoulder. He was wobbling as he appeared to be telling her something important while staring at the beginning of her cleavage. She laughed, picked up an empty bottle from the half wall that separated the pool table from the dance floor, and walked off. Teddy was glad the Marine's hand hadn't slid down to her ass. She'd told him after the one time he tried to intervene, *let it go or you'll get me fired*. He sometimes wondered what he was doing with her. And then she saw him and smiled big causing his doubt to melt away. She started towards him. She was petite, shapely, blue eyes, auburn hair, *too good for him*, he thought. But she'd given herself to him, which tended to erase those doubts too. And the fact she had reassured him that these other guys were wasting their time, or so he hoped.

"So, what are my two favorite Marines drinking tonight?"

Teddy put his hand in the small of her back, kind of like he'd seen Butch do to Olivia at the USO that night, but he did not pull her to him. He looked up leaving his hand where it was. "Give us a coupla Pabsts."

Maria's left hand dropped to the shoulder of Teddy's outstretched arm. It gave the appearance, as she had intended, that their connection was more than just drunken flirtation. Her expression became serious. "You'd tell me if you were leaving, wouldn't you?"

Teddy laughed. "Sure, I ain't going anywhere." He laughed some more. "Might be peelin' spuds but I'll be here till at least next spring."

She frowned. "I waited on a couple of guys earlier tonight. They were sergeants, I think. I heard one of them say that this time next week Pendleton will be a ghost town."

Teddy looked at Tony who shrugged. "They tend to not tell privates what's going on till they need some heavy lifting done."

It occurred to Teddy that as secretive as the big shots were, they might just wait until the last minute to spring it upon them that they were leaving. But then it came to him that he wasn't going anywhere when his unit left except to KP and Maria's bed on occasion. He gently squeezed her back. "Nobody's said boo to us about leavin'."

The fearful look on her face did not go away. "Well, it wasn't like these guys were advertising it."

Teddy looked at Maria and squeezed her back again. "I'll ask our sergeant tomorrow. He might give us the straight dope."

"Do that, I'd like to know."

Teddy smiled. "Even if we are leaving I won't be part of it, the Colonel said so."

Tony laughed. "You'll be a champion spud peeler come next spring."

And then Teddy noticed the bartender frowning in their direction. "You better go, Maria, your boss is giving us the stink eye."

Instinctively, she looked around which caused her boss to double down on his scowl. "I better get your order."

Teddy watched her go, drinking in her slender body hidden beneath loose-fitting black pants and a red blouse. His look was such that Tony laughed. "Hells – bells, you're worse 'n old love sick Hereford bull. 'Fore I know it you'll be pawing the floor and bellerin'."

A sheepish grin came to Teddy's face. "Shit." He paused and then went on. "She'd make a lotta guys paw the floor, don't ya think?"

Tony nodded. "I reckon so."

"I never dreamed I'd have a girl like her. Makes me have to pinch myself about twice a day just so I know this is all real."

"That's kinda the way I feel about my Emma Lou. She was the prettiest girl in our school and I ain't just saying that."

Teddy saw the homesick look in Tony's eyes. "I didn't think you were." He added, "She must get writer's cramp as many letters as you get."

They laughed, the bond of friendship being readily apparent to anyone watching.

And then Maria was back, her sweet perfume temporarily displacing the smell of smoke and spilled beer. "Here you go."

Teddy gave her a dollar. Beer was twenty-five cents a bottle. She started to make change. "Keep it."

She looked at him and smiled. "Thanks, Hon."

When she was out of earshot, Tony parroted, "Hon?"

Teddy glanced at Maria walking away and then came back to Tony. "That's the first time she's ever called me that."

He grinned, "She must be really smitten with you."

Teddy took a long drink of his beer. The carbonation caused his eyes to water followed by a mild belch. "Tips in here ain't good."

They each had two more beers while playing pool. Teddy gave Maria a kiss in spite of the nasty look the bartender was sending his way. She'd said, *come by tomorrow night and let me know what's going on*, to which he'd replied, *I will*.

Reveille had sounded some time ago and they were now standing in formation near their barracks. Teddy could tell right off that it wasn't going to be another routine training day. The captain was there, a short man with a black moustache and wire rim glasses. His demeanor was serious. "Men, today is the day. We're shipping out. We're going to war."

Panic momentarily seized Teddy's mind. *Maria was right but hey, I'll be here till spring.*

"This is the day we've prepared for, the day we can pay the Japs back for Pearl Harbor. We will be leaving from this location at 1000 hours. Be here with your combat gear and rifle at that time." He paused before continuing. "Between now and then you are not to leave the base or make any phone calls. Word will get out soon enough that we're leaving."

From within the ranks, a bold Marine called out, "Sir, where are going?"

"Your destination will be made known to you once you're at sea."

The arbitrary tone of the captain added to Teddy's uneasiness. He was no longer a naïve starry-eyed kid. He knew what he was getting into. Just the time at sea to wherever they were going would be miserable. And Maria, he would miss her and she him. But then his inner self took hold of his fear. *Soon as this formation is over, I need to go talk to Harper. This is a mistake. I'm not supposed to be going on this, not now anyway.*

The captain rambled on for a while longer. Teddy was oblivious to most of it being preoccupied with the thought playing over and over in his mind, *I'm not supposed to be part of this.* Further back in his mind his conscience pondered if he was a coward wanting to now play this card of him being too young to go into combat. But no, it was what the colonel had said. If Teddy got killed Gladys Wilson would be all over the colonel's ass.

And then it was over. They were free to go to chow before stripping their bunks down and packing their gear. Teddy thought, or hoped, that since Harper knew his situation he might seek him out, but he did not. Instead, he was like everybody else headed to breakfast. Teddy jogged to catch up. "Sarge, can I talk to you?"

Harper stopped. "What's up, Private?"

"Colonel King said I was supposed to be reassigned to a quartermaster outfit here on post? That I wouldn't ship out until I was old enough."

Harper's face was blank like he'd forgotten what was decided three months ago. Finally, he said, "King shipped out last month."

"Well, didn't he leave some paperwork for me?"

"Not that I know of."

The color left Teddy's face. "Isn't there somebody you can talk to?"

Harper snorted. "I don't know that you want to open that can of worms. King was going way out of bounds for you. Anybody else would have thrown your ass out of the Corps."

Teddy appeared dumbfounded. "So, I -"

Harper cut in, "So, either you go along on our little camping trip in the South Pacific or go home. You signed up to be a Marine. Here's your chance. If you want out, let me know after chow. Otherwise, pack your shit." And with that Harper walked off.

Teddy was standing there watching Harper strut off at a brisk pace when Tony came next to him. "So, what did he say?"

"There ain't gonna be any peelin' spuds."

"What?"

"King's deal is off. Harper says if I bring it up now, they'll kick me out."

"What are you gonna do?"

Teddy sighed heavily. "I don't know. It'd be a chance to stay here with Maria."

"You'd have almost two years before you'd be old enough for the draft."

Teddy came back quick. There was a hint of irritation in his voice. "I wouldn't be doing it to get outta fightin' the Japs."

"There 'll be those that won't see it that way. They'll question why you brought up your age now. They'll think-" Tony went silent not wanting to create tension between them.

"They'll think I'm afraid, that I'm a coward."

For a time, Teddy's words hung in the air waiting for Tony to refute them, but he did not. Instead, he came back, "We're all afraid."

"So, if you was me, what would you do?"

"You know I ain't anxious to do this."

"You'd take the out?"

Tony shook his head. "People take note of who served and who didn't."

It popped into Teddy's mind that Pete's time in the Marines had kept Jimmy Polson's dad from calling the sheriff on him. And it may have been the reason George Phillips had hired an ex-con when no one else would. On his slate of life's accomplishments, Pete had only one entry, he served in the war. Teddy sighed. "Looks like I ain't got a choice."

Tony flashed a wry grin. "Oh, you've got one. It just isn't good."

CHAPTER THIRTY-THREE

At one point, Teddy had made it almost to the USO where they had pay phones. He'd decided two things. One, there'd be shame come his way if he played the age card now. And two, order or not, he was going to call Maria before they left. It was fixed in his mind that he would gain some solace if he explained to her why he had to go. Then, out of nowhere, came Harper. *If I can't call my wife, you damned sure can't call your girl.*

Their ship had not left until almost dark. Teddy stood at the railing. The lights of San Diego were just barely visible now. His mind was tied in worry knots. *By now she'll know I'm not coming. She'll probably ask some Marine if my unit shipped out. And if he's drunk enough, he'll tell her and if he's not he'll tell her anyway and offer to take my place.*

"You gonna sleep up here?"

Teddy looked over as Tony stepped up and rested his forearms on the railing. "Probably be better than that sardine can below."

"Bunks five deep. Can you believe that shit?"

"At least we got the second and third levels. Can you feature that poor slob up on the fifth. You 'bout need a rope to pull yourself up there."

Tony lit a cigarette and tossed the match away. He took a thoughtful drag looking down at the dark water. "Damn, the sea is powerful. As big as this boat is it ain't nuthin' for it to lift us up."

Teddy said, the queasiness in his voice apparent, "Don't remind me."

"Sorry."

"I'm already seasick. That's why I'm up here. The fresh air helps a little."

"You know you got to be in your bunk by 2200?"

Teddy nodded. "Yeah, I ain't lookin' forward to it. Already smells like sweat and farts down there."

Abruptly, the speaker above them blared. "Marines, this is Colonel Gibson. I hope you're settled in as comfortably as the situation will allow. Be patient, this is only temporary. Depending upon the weather and the sea, our journey will take about ten days."

Teddy groaned. "Oh, shit." But he was not the only one to grumble. Men to either side of him and Tony could be heard.

Gibson continued. "Our destination is Guadalcanal." Another round of excited voices sounded in the darkness.

"Your fellow Marines are putting it to the Japs, but they are a tenacious enemy. So, we're going to lend a hand. I will keep you apprised as information becomes available. Get some sleep. You'll be glad you did in the days ahead."

"I ain't got a sliver of an idea where this place is at, do you?" asked Teddy.

Tony took a casual draw on his cigarette and blew the smoke out. "Never heard of it till just now. I suppose it's another speck of land in the midst of all this water that the big shots have decided is worth dying for."

Teddy leaned back from the rail. "I think I'm gonna go write a letter to Maria before they turn the lights out."

Tony laughed. "Where do you think it'll go?"

It then dawned on Teddy where they were. "Oh, yeah."

"There'll be plenty of time for that over the next ten days. Hell, you could write her a book by then." Tony took a final draw on his cigarette and flicked it into the sea. "I'm going to bed."

"I ain't going down there any sooner than I have to."

"Alright, see you in the morning."

The lights on shore were almost gone. Teddy moved his eyes up the coast to Pendleton. His mind's eye taunted him. First it envisioned Maria at work, sad that he had not come and in the next instant, she was angry and indifferent and flirting with a new Marine. And then he cursed himself, *dammit I should have told Harper I wanted out.*

It was the 14th of September when they finally dropped anchor off Guadalcanal. They'd arrived in the night and were told to get some rest, that they'd be going ashore at first light. The sound of gunfire and explosions excluded the possibility of sleeping, at least for Teddy it did. At 0300 they were awakened. To feed a thousand men takes time. The Navy cooks had been up since midnight peeling spuds, frying pork chops, mixing powdered eggs and making gallons and gallons of coffee.

Tony carved out a bite of meat and forked it into his mouth. "Not bad chow."

From across the table Teddy nodded as he picked at his food.

Tony came back. "Better eat up. Gonna be C-rats on the island."

Teddy looked at him eating and shook his head. "I don't see how you can pack it away like that knowing we could be dead before noon."

"Didn't you hear the Colonel last night? The Japs are on the run. We're here to mop up."

"He also said, *don't let your guard down.*"

Tony frowned. "Well, I'm looking forward to getting off this damned boat and I ain't gonna go hungry."

"Well, I agree with you on getting' off the boat. I'm sick of being sick."

"There ya go, a bright spot to the morning."

Teddy took a bite of pork chop. "Mailed my letter to Maria last night."

Tony grinned. "This boat will probably ride a little higher in the water after the mailman has come for it."

"Look who's talkin'. I saw that dictionary you mailed Emma Lou."

Tony's face reddened a little. "You ever wonder if it was you doing the waiting if you'd give in to it?"

"I like to think I wouldn't."

"We ain't got much choice out here."

"But you're saying, if we was back home in Montana, would we be true?"

"Exactly, it's a scary thought."

Teddy paused for a moment. "Maybe for you."

Tony laughed. "We'll see if a year from now some rotten crotch in a bar somewhere doesn't tempt you."

Out of nowhere Sergeant Harper appeared at the end of their table. His eyes conveyed the sarcasm even before he spoke. "You two gold bricks waiting for bingo to start or what? Eat up. You've got a prior engagement this morning, in case you forgot. Two minutes and I better not see either one of you here."

Teddy watched Harper walk away. He was still of the belief that if Harper had helped he could have gotten reassigned at Pendleton. He whispered, mostly so Tony could read his lips, "What an asshole."

In less than two minutes they were gone from the dining area and some three hours later they were finally in a Higgins boat headed to shore. A canopy of rain clouds, thick and dark, hung overhead. As it worked out they were near the front of the boat, not far from Harper. A fine mist, in sync with the lunging of the boat, came over the ramp. No one complained. Teddy could see columns of smoke well beyond the beach. He was about to point them out to Tony when he noticed Harper and the Lieutenant were looking at them too. The Lieutenant said, loud enough to be heard over the boat's engine, "The Japs counter attacked last night."

Harper nodded like it was no big deal. "We'll give 'em hell, Sir."

Teddy gripped his rifle tighter wondering if it was wise not having a round chambered. But that was the order, not until they were out of the boat and had a visible target. Harper had been emphatic about it.

And then the boat surged to a halt and the ramp dropped. Harper was first out. "Let's go men."

At first they ran and then they saw there were other Marines at the tree line, probably more reason to not have a round chambered. Some of them were smiling. All of them were dirty. Eventually, they were directed to an area within the camp and told to dig in. *Make 'em deep, boys. Might be what saves your ass.*

By 1700 Teddy and Tony had finished their foxhole. It was deep enough that they could stand up in it. They'd even put a roof, of sorts, on it by laying two logs across the dirt they'd mounded up around the hole. They could see out to shoot while hopefully a Jap grenade wouldn't fall through. However, a direct hit by a mortar or artillery round would make the whole effort pointless.

They'd just opened some C-rations, per Corporal Wilkens say so, when Teddy saw Harper coming towards them. He acted like he hadn't seen him and whispered, "Sarge is coming."

Tony mumbled. "Ah, shit."

And then he was there, having had plenty of time to see what a good job they'd done on their foxhole. It was obvious too, the sweat stains and dirt on their utilities. They naively expected that he would compliment them. "Where's Wilkens?"

Teddy nodded towards a patch of tall brush. "Went to the latrine. Something gave him the trots."

Harper frowned. "When he comes back have him come see me. Our platoon is setting up an ambush tonight."

Teddy's heart instantly ratcheted up. He knew better than to say anything but, "Ok, Sarge."

A derisive grin came to Harper's face. "And to think you could've been a civilian right now cozied up to that girl of yours. Instead, here you are bunkin' with Halverson." He then looked at the both of them and laughed and kept on laughing as he walked away.

It was Tony's turn to confirm it. "That guy is an asshole."

CHAPTER THIRTY-FOUR

The jungle was engulfed in heavy shadow. In Teddy's estimation it would have qualified as dark had it not been for a faint awareness of light in the direction of the sun's retreat. But on they went as stealthy as forty men can be on an overgrown two-track that snaked through the jungle. The thought hammered in Teddy's head, *who's ambushing who?* All around them it was quiet. As they'd left camp a grungy looking Marine who'd obviously been in the fight shouted, *watch out for the woodpeckers.* Teddy thought he was trying to be funny until another guy told him that *woodpecker* was what they called a particular Jap machine gun on account of the way it sounded. A longways off to his right he could hear staccato gunfire, different than their machine guns. He thought, *maybe that's a woodpecker.* His mind immediately ginned up an image of the damage the woodpecker was doing. The exchange was lopsided with the woodpecker doing most of the shooting. Even though it was warm and humid a shiver ran through Teddy as his mind's eye saw Marines dying. Suddenly, the woodpecker paused. To clear a jam, get more ammo, Teddy didn't know. But then the Garands began firing, lots of them. His mind went back to Pendleton and how they'd practiced it. *There's the base fire makin' that gun crew hide their heads.* And then he could see them, more Marines, just as plain as if he was there with them. They were maneuvering on the woodpecker, grenades at the ready. *Any second now those boys will be going to Jap heaven.*

Suddenly, the woodpecker opened up, except this one wasn't far away. There was screaming and yelling but mostly it was the clatter of the woodpecker. Near the middle of the column the Lieutenant shouted, "Fall back, fall back." Men, wide eyed and terrified were running towards Teddy, echoing the Lieutenant's command.

Teddy said aloud to no one, "Shit, we've been ambushed." And then he heard it, he saw it, bullets ripping holes in the big leaves around him. The woodpecker was relentless, unmerciful. It wanted to kill him for no other reason than he was an American. Teddy had never thought about it in its rawest form that these people, not knowing a thing about him, wanted to kill him. It didn't make sense.

Harper shouted, "Take cover off the road to your left."

Teddy crouched and followed the others into the dense, almost impenetrable, vegetation. What had been the Lieutenant's excuse for staying on the road was now to be their savior. There was some panic among the men, kids in a civilized world. Harper hissed, "Shut the hell up." Instantly, they complied save for one of the wounded. He'd been shot in the stomach and could not suppress his moans. Some were laying on the ground, others on one knee, but all of them were looking in the direction of the Japs and the men they'd left on the road. Harper, on the other hand, was standing taking count of how many had survived. He looked at the Lieutenant, crouched, balancing himself with his M-1 Carbine. "Twenty-seven, Sir. That includes three wounded."

The Lieutenant frowned. "Means we've got 13 people out there."

"We've got to flank 'em, Sir, and do it before they do it to us."

The Lieutenant looked into the jungle where the Japs were hiding. It was impossible to see more than 20 or 30 feet in most places. He shook his head. "They'll hear us coming."

"We don't have a choice."

He sighed in disgust. "We'll leave our wounded, Doc and two men here. The rest of us will get on line and sweep up this side of the road to that Jap gun. We need to stay aware of the men next to one another. We don't want to be shooting ourselves."

Harper relayed the order adding, "keep sight of the man next to you."

Teddy was resistant to the fact that Tony was probably dead. A few minutes ago, when his heart was on the verge of exploding with fear, he'd had little time to think about it. But now, as they crept through the jungle the relative strangers to either side of him were a constant reminder that he'd never be able to share things with his best friend. And it was all because of Harper ordering Tony to walk point.

In the near darkness Teddy strained to see. He kept his eyes straight ahead dissecting every element of his surroundings to be sure they belonged. All the while in his mind the naysayer shouted over and over, *this is bullshit. First you'll know there's a Jap out there is when his bullet plows into your chest.* Suddenly, he felt alone and looked for the man on his left, Seifert, he thought was his name. They made eye contact. The fear in them, all of them, was palpable. He paused to look for the man on his right and that's when he saw it, a muzzle flash off to his right but out in front of him. In that same instant, he saw from the corner of his eye the man on line also to his right crumple like a rag doll. Teddy didn't recall making the decision to shoot. The next thing he knew his M1 Garand was bucking into his shoulder again and again and again until the empty clip popped out with its distinctive ping. He dropped to one knee to reload all the while staring hard at where he'd seen the muzzle flash. His inner voice cried out. *I got that sonovabitch.* From behind him he heard heavy breathing the equal of his own. He jerked around, pushing a new clip into the magazine of his rifle.

"Easy Walker."

Teddy lowered his rifle and allowed Harper to approach on his hands and knees. He whispered, his voice was quivery. "I think I got one, Sarge. Over there."

"You see 'im fall?"

"No, I just shot where he fired from."

Harper scowled and shook his head. He looked over at Seifert. "Cover us." He stood to a crouch, his rifle at the ready. "Let's see what you got."

Teddy led the way trembling from the inside out. He was moving slow and quiet, his eyes fixed on where he thought the dead Jap would be. Not ever having a real father around, he'd never gone hunting let alone kill anything. The closest he'd come was right after Tom had married Agnes, he was feeling fatherly then and had taken Teddy to shoot cans and bottles. He'd said they'd go hunting, but they never did. And now here he was, walking up on his first kill. He was within five feet of the big leafy plant before it suddenly registered that for the past several seconds he'd been looking at fingers in the detritus beneath the branches. His adrenaline surge was such he instantly raised his rifle and came close to firing. And then he whispered, his voice shaking, "Here he is, Sarge."

"Freeze, Walker. I've heard these little bastards will play dead till you get right up to 'em and then they'll pull the pin on a grenade." Harper stepped around Teddy towards the body,

Teddy had never seen a dead body before. He felt relieved that Harper would be first to see it.

The Sergeant went behind the big leaves, his rifle aimed at the body. Very soon, he lowered it. "He's dead."

Teddy made eye contact with Harper. *How could he be sure that quick unless it's bad, bloody, gruesome?* He knew what was expected but his legs would not move. He felt like he was going to be sick.

To his credit, the Sergeant didn't call for Teddy to come over. "You got him good, Walker. I think he was a lookout for the gun up the road. Keep people from sneakin' up on 'em." He looked away towards where a corpsman was kneeling beside the dead Marine whose name Teddy didn't remember. And then he looked down to where the dead Jap had fired from. He shook his head. "Poor sap. Point blank range. He didn't have a chance." Harper sighed. "Alright, Walker, let's move out."

Harper motioned to the corpsman and Seifert to move on, they in turn signaled down the line to go forward.

Teddy had no choice but to un-freeze his legs. He still felt sick and weak. And so, he was surprised when his legs took him right by the vegetation that hid the soldier he had killed. He could have chosen to veer away, but for some inexplicable reason his legs betrayed him. From the corner of his eye it was instantly apparent why Harper knew the Jap was dead. There was matter protruding from the top of his head. In the poor light its color contrasted with the black hair surrounding it. As much as Teddy wanted to turn away there was a part of him that was shouting out, *you did this. You should at least be man enough to look at what you've done.* His guilt caused him to pause and turn so he could better accept the consequences of his actions. He was processing this, fighting back against his conscience, telling himself that the dead Jap had brought this on himself when, from out of the darkness, he was punched in the right side of his back. It was a jolt like none other that he'd received in life. Much harder than when Tom had smacked him at supper that night. His knees were buckling when the crack of the Jap 7.7 Arisaka rifle finally reached his ears. He recognized immediately what had just happened and the likelihood of what was to follow. His inner self whimpered, *I don't wanna die.* He fell, his face not more than two feet from the dead Jap's face. The mouth agape, eyes wide open, shocked at being dead. Teddy was repulsed but he could not move. The pain was immense. All around him he could hear firing. Lots of it. He could do nothing but lay there staring back at the man he had killed. He wondered if the chaplain was right. People had spirits and now this guy's spirit was there laughing at him. And then it occurred to him that maybe spirits could travel in the blink of an eye and that Agnes and Pete were there right now just waiting for him to cross over.

CHAPTER THIRTY-FIVE

In sufficient quantity, pain can render a person oblivious to what's going on around them. It was fortunate for Teddy that he had reached this point early in the fight and even more so that the corpsman had plenty of morphine. Now, however, he had an awareness that somebody was looking at him. Reluctantly, he nudged his eyes open.

"It's about time you woke up."

Teddy gave himself a moment to gain his wits as so far they appeared to be playing a trick on him. The last thing he recalled was being visited by spirits. Finally, he said, "I thought you was dead."

Tony snorted. "So, did the Japs."

Teddy managed a weak grin, still struggling to untangle himself from the cobweb of anesthesia. "Where'd they get ya?"

Tony turned so Teddy could better see the right side of his head and leaned down. He laughed. "Doc says I might have a permanent part in my hair. The hell of it is I don't part it on this side."

They both laughed, but not too hard. Teddy said the obvious. "Shit, Tony, another quarter inch and you'd be a goner."

He shook his head. "If that Jap had taken time to aim instead of spraying the road, I'd probably be worm food."

Teddy came back in a somber tone. "How'd the fight go?"

"When the rest of the platoon started movin' in the Japs just slunk away. Harper thinks there wasn't more than a squad of them."

"So, we got the worst of it?"

Tony looked around to see who might be listening in the big tent of wounded, he then lowered his voice. "Hell yeah, we did. Walkin' down that old road like we was. Ten dead Marines and four wounded on day one. You should be thankful you've got a ticket out of here."

Teddy remained quiet. They both did, listening for a time to the American flag outside whip and flutter in the afternoon wind. As if to compliment the flag, the heavy green canvas of the tent's roof heaved and sighed. Its odor struck Teddy as musty and oily but nonetheless soothing. Strangely enough, the possibility of leaving this made him sad. At least right here and right now it did. And Tony, he was like the brother he never had. In the next instant, though, the critic in his mind shouted, *maybe Tony feels guilty for not seeing the woodpecker and warning the platoon so now he is blaming the Lieutenant for being on the road.* Shame prompted him to speak lest the silence say something else. "I suspect there'll be lots of scuttlebutt on the wisdom of walking down that road."

"You can bet your sweet ass on that," Tony paused before adding, "Because that's exactly what it'll cost you if we do that again."

The flaps at the far end of the tent parted and a Navy Corpsman entered. Spying Tony, he started at a brisk pace between the rows of cots toward him and Teddy. Knowing that he wasn't supposed to be there, Tony went first. "I was just leaving."

The corpsman, late twenties and stocky, came back straight faced, "That's good. This man needs his rest."

Tony grinned like a mischievous schoolboy. "I'll try to drop by tomorrow, after you're rested up."

Teddy noted the scowl on the corpsman's face and smiled. "I'll see you then."

Oblivious to Tony's departure, the corpsman studied Teddy's chart. "Gunshot wound to the chest. Umm, you're lucky, been on the other side it would have hit your heart."

It came to Teddy's mind. *Maybe if Ma had shot Tom on the right side he would have lived, just like me and so would her and Pete.*

"Have you experienced any headache, nausea or vomiting?"

"I got a little of the first two but no throwing up."

"It's the anesthesia they gave you during surgery. I'll give you something for the headache. You feel alright otherwise?"

"My chest hurts."

"Well, that comes with getting shot."

Teddy thought, *what a smartass,* but he kept it to himself.

The corpsman added, "In a little while you can have some morphine."

"But not now?"

"You've already had a lot. Try to get some rest. You'll be leaving here soon."

"Leaving? Where too?"

"Initially, a hospital ship. After that I'm not sure. New Zealand, Pearl Harbor, I don't know. Most likely, the war's over for you."

"Over?"

"You're gonna be on the mend for a while."

"What's a while?"

"Depends on how it goes, but I would think four or five months."

"In bed?"

The corpsman became irritated. "You need to ask the doctor these questions. He'll be around later tonight."

Before Teddy could respond, their attention was diverted to artillery fire not far away. First came the sharp report of the cannon separated by only a few seconds of silence before the dull explosion of the round landing. The corpsman shook his head. "Damned Japs." He started to leave and then, sensing Teddy staring at him, he paused, "Sometimes we go to bunkers and sometimes not. I'll be back if that's what we're doing." And then he walked out.

Teddy looked up at the gentle pulsations of the canvas. Had the artillery not started it would have been calming, maybe even coaxed him to sleep. Now, he lay there wondering if his luck was going to run out and a shell would find his tent. The corpsman did not return, at least not before the artillery subsided. When he did return it was with Teddy's supper and news. In the morning he would be taken by Higgins boat out to a hospital ship to go where, the corpsman didn't know. Teddy did not press him on the matter. Instead, he savored the fact he hadn't been blown up by the artillery. He wondered too, if the chaplain's prayer back at Pendleton was working for him or if he was getting by on luck.

Because a corpsman would be doing a walk-through at the top of every hour, two gas lanterns, evenly spaced, had been hung from the aluminum ridge pole that supported the apex part of the tent. Although they had been turned down low, they still emitted a steady hissing and an occasional sputtering like they wanted to quit. One of the lanterns was located straight out from Teddy. He'd alternated staring at the intense white flame trapped inside its glass globe and the clear liquid in the glass bottle hanging from a metal stand beside his cot. An IV tapped to the back of his right hand was slowly draining the bottle.

At first Teddy thought he was dreaming. Whispered voices, a whimper, a moan unrestrained and finally, "Oh, damn that hurts."

When he'd fallen asleep the cots to either side of him had been empty. Now, the one to his left was occupied. The wounded man uttered a sigh, a groan to which one of the two corpsmen standing there responded, "I'll come back later." And then he and the other one headed for the tent flaps barely slowing as they brushed through them.

"I believe those guys have had their fill of me for today."

This far from the lantern, the light had become soft and near yellow. Nonetheless, Teddy saw who it was. "How ya makin' it, Billy?"

"Not worth a dam."

"Sorry to hear that. You were one of the ones that got machine gunned on the road?"

"Yeah," he labored as he adjusted to his side so he could better see Teddy. "The sonsabitches shot my leg off."

Teddy could see that the thin green wool blanket had collapsed where Billy's right leg from about the knee down should have been. He said again, "Sorry to hear that."

Billy forced a laugh. "I heard a sniper killed you."

"He tried."

Billy snorted. "Yeah, yesterday was not a good day to show up to work. Being on that road was like shootin' fish in a barrel for the Japs."

Laying there looking at Billy, a Nevada cowboy with half a leg gone, made Teddy appreciate only having a hole clear through his chest. He came back. "It was a rough go, no doubt about it." He thought to add, *but we've got our tickets home.* Fortunately, he caught himself when it occurred to him that Billy would likely trade his ticket for the leg he lost.

They talked on into the night until somebody on the other side of the room hollered, "Hey, you two old hens wanna put a cork in it."

Billy gave an audible sigh. "I guess that's our cue."

"Yeah, I'll see ya in the morning."

Teddy went quiet, staring up at the shadowy light that had collided with the tent's roof. In it he did not see the usual parade of characters from home. Tonight, there were just two competing for attention. Maria, who generally prevailed was mostly off stage. She'd aged him like only a woman can. He no longer felt uneasy when Marine stories and boasts went there. He was confident, though, that he would never share his time with her. She was deserving of better. Her successor for attention, however, was even more compelling. Teddy suspected he always would be. From the time that he'd awakened from the anesthesia this afternoon until now there'd never been more than a few minutes in a row when he couldn't see the dead Jap. It was like spirits could invade a person's mind and this guy was getting his revenge. *Kill me will you. You'll rue the day you ever saw me.* He taunted Teddy, on and on, long after the bottle hanging by his bed had gone dry.

Sleep had been a long time in pushing the dead Jap out and now they were taking it away. They said it was because a storm was coming that they'd rousted him with the chickens. By 0700 he was laying on a stretcher in the bottom of a Higgins boat next to Billy and at 0815 they were in real beds on board a hospital ship. Regardless of their motives, Teddy had not gotten to see Tony before leaving. It was like he'd barely gotten a taste of Guadalcanal and the war. and it was now spitting him out.

CHAPTER THIRTY-SIX

On the 24th of October they finally reached Pearl Harbor. It had been a miserable trip for Teddy as, in addition to being seasick, his wound had become infected. For a time his temperature had gotten dangerously high and although he'd been too incoherent Billy later told him, *those doctors were standing right there talking about you like you were already a goner. I know they was surprised when you didn't die on 'em.*

By the middle of November both Teddy and Billy's condition had improved considerably. With permission, they were allowed to go outside and get some sun in the hospital flower garden. It had lots of colorful flowers, big red orchids being Teddy's favorite. It was intended as a place where patients could relax and maybe forget about the war for a while. In that regard, it was only partially successful for Teddy.

Billy was sitting in a white wooden Adirondack chair shading his eyes with both hands while studying two ships just barely visible on the horizon. "You think the Japs 'd be nervy enough to just steam right in here in broad daylight a second time and shoot things up?"

Teddy gave no credence to Billy's idle comment as he was preoccupied with writing another letter to Maria. Several seconds went by while he finished the sentence he had just started before he looked at Billy. "I'm thinkin' if we even let'em get close to here again we might be deserving of what we get."

Billy reached for a pack of Lucky Strikes on the small table next to his chair, shook one out and lit it. He drew on it and then blew the smoke out all the while looking at Teddy who had gone back to writing. "This is pretty swell duty, don't ya think?"

"Umm- uh."

"Kind of like being on vacation."

"Yeah."

Billy looked at the distant boats like he was bored and puffed on his cigarette again. "Did I tell ya, I'm getting' my leg this week? Doc says maybe by Thursday."

"That'll be great."

Billy laughed. "I told him I just wanted a peg leg so I could always be a pirate on Halloween. He didn't think that was very funny."

Teddy laughed, mostly to be polite.

And then it came, maybe out of boredom or stagnant thoughts. He knew better. "So, have you heard from Maria yet?"

A cocktail of hurt and anger flushed through Teddy's mind. It lit what was now a short fuse. "Billy, you know damned good and well I ain't got a letter from her. You were right there with me at mail call yesterday."

"Well, you got a letter."

"From Tony. I even told you that he said things was going alright for him on the Canal."

"Sorry, guess I need to pay attention."

Teddy sighed and shook his head. "No, I shouldn't have jumped on you. I just don't understand why she's not answering my letters. Hell, I've written her eight or nine times since we've been at Pearl."

Billy appeared at a loss for words. Finally, he smiled and said, "Maybe today will be the day."

Teddy collected his writing materials and stood up. "I'm gonna lay down for a while. Feelin'kinda tired." And with that he went inside.

At 1500 mail was distributed. By now the mail guy, a young sailor, knew who Teddy was. He didn't even slow as he went by Teddy's bed. There'd been times in the past when he'd pause to say, *sorry, Walker, nothing today*. And there'd been a time or two when Teddy had shamelessly asked him to check his bag again. But not today.

On Thursday Billy was fitted for his new leg. Right away he began practicing walking just like the doctor had instructed. First with crutches to get the feel of it. Within a few days he had his balance without the crutches but more than anything, he had a smile. Teddy attributed it to the fact Billy had a girl back home in Elko that wrote him on a regular basis. In her last letter she had suggested they get married knowing full well that he'd be a one-legged cowboy. Teddy's envy was such that he'd come to seriously think, *I'd trade a leg for a letter from Maria with a marriage proposal.* But none came. Nonetheless, time in paradise rolled on until somehow it had gotten to be the 20th of December and they had received their orders.

With the edge of his fork, Billy cut into his second stack of hotcakes. He shoveled it in while looking at Teddy and chewed enough so he could talk. "You suppose Teresa will be put off sleepin' with a guy that's only got one and half legs?"

Teddy grinned. "You still got all the parts that matter."

Billy laughed but not for long. "You don't think she'll be sorry of her bargain once she sees me and maybe when she has a chance to compare me to guys with two legs."

Teddy shook his head. "No, no I don't. I think she really cares about you."

"I do too, but sometimes I wonder if she just feels sorry for me."

"From what you've told me about her, she don't sound like that kind of person."

Billy sighed wanting even more reassurance, "You just never know about people."

"Dammit, Billy, she ain't a Maria. Just go home to her and be glad you got her."

A look of awareness that he'd hit a sore spot came to Billy's face. "Sorry, didn't mean to bring that up."

"You didn't, I did."

"You know what I mean."

"I do, you just never can tell about some people. Maria is one of 'em, your girl isn't."

CHAPTER THIRTY-SEVEN

Their plane landed in San Diego on the 21st of December. For Billy, his time in the Marines would end right there. Teddy, on the other hand, was going on to Pendleton even though he had seven days of Christmas leave.

"You should just come home with me," urged Billy. "You can meet my family and Teresa and my mother will feed you like a hog going to market."

On the surface Billy's offer was tempting, but it had barely settled in Teddy's mind when he saw the potential pain it might cause. It'd be a constant reminder that Billy had everything he wanted, a family and a girl that loved him. And there'd be the questions about his family like he was from normal people that hadn't been killed in a court room shootout. Teddy could see how it'd likely unfold just plain as day. "I appreciate the offer, Billy, but I believe I'll stick around here."

Billy frowned as the words escaped him. "And do what, go looking for Maria?"

Teddy snorted seeing himself as pathetic as maybe Billy was. "I don't know why, but yeah, that's probably what I'm gonna do."

The futility of saying anything to the contrary was apparent to both of them. Billy extended his hand. "Stay in touch. You ever get an itch to come to Nevada you're always welcome."

Teddy shook Billy's hand, saying only, "I'll do that." He paused, while drawing a wry face, and then added, "I'd invite you to Montana, but you know my situation."

Billy nodded. "Semper fie."

Teddy responded in kind and then they went their separate ways, Billy into a two-story building to get his discharge and Teddy to the bus stop. He'd barely sat down on the bus when he began to question his decision. *What do I say to her? It's no coincidence that she hasn't written me back. But why? That's all I want to know.* He knew though that even if he were to find this out, it wouldn't ease the hurt he felt.

There was a scheduled stop four blocks from the Rusty Bucket. Teddy got off and started towards the bar. After two blocks with his heavy sea bag hanging from his left shoulder he realized that he wasn't his old self, that he still needed to heal. He laughed, thinking, *now the Corps makes me a spud peeler. Just needed to get shot in the chest first.*

It was raucous inside the bar, just as Teddy had remembered it except Maria wasn't there. He dropped his sea bag in the corner of the room nearest the door. The bartender whose first name he'd learned was Kenny, saw him coming. He said, from some distance, in a loud indifferent voice, "She's gone."

Teddy stepped next to the bar so as to not have to shout. Inwardly, he hoped too that Kenny the civilian would recognize the ribbons on his chest, especially the one indicating that he had shed blood. But even if he did, he suspected Kenny would continue being the 4F jerk that he was. Teddy came back, "Where'd she go?"

"She left town with one of your buddies."

"My buddy?"

"Had a green suit just like you."

"And you don't know where they went?"

"No, I didn't care."

A barmaid to Teddy's left who'd been unloading empty glasses from her tray and pretending not to eavesdrop cut in. "Why don't you tell him, Kenny? Why be an asshole about it?"

Kenny scoffed sarcastically, "Ok, you give him the good news."

Teddy's heart jumped like it was out of sync. It caused him to take a breath. He looked at the barmaid. "So, what's the good news?"

She nodded to an empty table against the wall. "Let's sit down."

Kenny held up two fingers and glared at her. "Two minutes."

The barmaid who was frumpy with red hair and a chipped front tooth gave him a hateful look before walking away. Teddy followed.

They'd just sat down when she began. "You must be Teddy."

It may have been the crow's feet at the corners of her eyes or a few streaks of gray hair that prompted him to come back respectfully, "Yes, Ma'am."

"My name's Louise."

Teddy nodded. "Pleased to meet you."

She went right to it. "I don't think Maria meant to hurt you. It just worked out that way."

"So, where is she?"

"She moved back east with a Marine."

"Where?"

"Camp Lejune. She said she'd write but so far she hasn't."

Teddy sighed and shook his head. "I thought I meant something to her."

"She thought the same thing about you, but when you left without coming to say goodbye or even calling that hurt at first, then it made her mad."

"I tried to call but they wouldn't let me."

"Well, the first letter she got was in November. By then it was too late. Pretty girls like her don't last long with this many men around."

Teddy did the math in his head and became angry, "Two months without a letter and she takes up with another guy?"

For a few seconds Louise said nothing allowing Teddy to hear himself. She came back, "What would you do? What was she to think?"

Inwardly Teddy cursed. *Damned military can't even deliver a letter on time.* Aloud, he said what was most likely a lie, "I'd a waited till I knew for sure."

"Well, I guess you had the stronger love."

"I guess I did."

A sudden uneasiness came into Louise's eyes. Teddy sensed she was almost eager to reveal its cause. And then she did. "When she left, Maria thought she was pregnant."

Louise's words were chilling to Teddy. Here he was not yet 17 years old, been to war and killed a man and still these words rocked him. "Does her new beau know this?"

"I don't think so."

Now hateful, Teddy scoffed, "It'll be the end of them when he finds out."

A distant, cold look overtook her face. "Probably, that's how men are."

From behind the bar, Kenny shouted, "Time's up."

Louise abruptly stood, her fear of pushing Kenny too far now more evident. She looked down at Teddy, her eyes suggesting that she cared. "Whaddaya drinkin'?"

Well, before now he'd been directing his anger at the *Bucket.* He blamed the drinking and drunkenness for how things had gone in his absence. Now, here he was about to be a part of it again. He thought to hold firm, but then his inner voice reminded him, *it'll just be you and a few other sad sacks in the barracks tonight.* And then his mind's eye, which could be blunt and cruel, shouted out, *Maria's not pining away for you. Why, right now she's probably in bed with this other guy.* And, as if this were not enough, an image of her pleasuring the guy appeared. Teddy retaliated, like he'd heard Pete tell it one time in a drinking story, "Gimme a double of Old Grandad with a water back."

"Why don't you be nice to yourself?"

Even though he'd never had a shot of hard liquor in his life, Teddy put forth his best cavalier face. "I am."

Louise shook her head. "You'll be sorry."

Teddy continued his façade with a laugh. "We'll see."

After the first drink, Louise refused to bring Teddy any more hard liquor. Undeterred, he went to the bar and ordered. 4F Kenny, being resentful of all the macho Marines, continued pouring in spite of Louise's objections. About midnight, Teddy fell off his bar stool, struggled to get up and then puked on the floor. He then fell face first into the mess he had created.

Kenny screamed over the bar, "You drunken sonovabitch."

Louise countered. "Well, what did you think was going to happen? You been giving it to him all night like it was ice water."

"He asked for it."

"You better hope the MPs don't come by here and question how a young Marine was allowed to get this drunk."

"Get him out of here."

Louise looked at the bartender with disgust and said sarcastically. "Sure, Kenny, I'll do that."

With help from another Marine, she rolled Teddy over and used a bar towel to swab the vomit from his face and the ribbons on his chest. Several Marines just out of boot camp but fully aware of what the ribbon for a purple heart looked like, carried Teddy out to the back seat of Louise's car.

CHAPTER THIRTY-EIGHT

It was 0215. An awareness that someone was tugging on his arm was beginning to register.

"C'mon, Teddy, you've got to help me. I can't lift you."

Teddy's mind was in a total fog. His first impulse was that he was dreaming. And then the tugs became stronger accompanied by grunts and strained whimpering. "Dammit Teddy, if you don't get up, you're sleeping in the car."

Suddenly, the fog began to lift, not because of the tugging or pleading but rather a wave of nausea. It was the equal of anything he'd experienced at sea. His eyes opened and he pushed himself upright in the seat. He gagged.

Louise shrieked. "No, Teddy. Not in my car."

It was almost like they'd rehearsed it, Louise abruptly stepping to the side and Teddy launching himself onto his hands and knees in the grass next to the driveway. He began to retch.

She laughed. "How ya likin' that Old Grandad now?"

Sensations other than the nausea and throbbing in his head were coming to him. He could feel the coolness of the grass under the palms of his hands. By the moonlight he could see from the corner of his eye Louise's brown and white saddleback oxfords. The laces were tied in bows, neat and crisp. *They're to Corps standards*, he thought. And then he retched again. He moaned, "Oh, do you have a gun? Just shoot me."

Louise laughed. "No, this is a valuable lesson. You need to remember it."

Teddy raised to his knees, tentative, looking around. The house in front of him was colorful, yellow with brown trim, small and simple. Bushes and flowers crowded either side of the front door. He ran the back of his hand across his mouth before speaking. "This your place?"

"I pay the rent."

In better light, a person could see that the paint was peeling and the living room picture window was cracked from top to bottom. But even in good light, compared to what Teddy was used to, it was a palace. "It's nice."

Louise stopped short of laughing when she saw that he was sincere. She moved on. "Can you walk?"

Old Grandad was slowly loosening its grip on Teddy. "Help me to my feet and we'll find out."

Louise took hold of his left arm around the bicep and lifted. The world was no longer spinning as fast. He thought to tell her, *I can make it on my own*. But then she just started out with a two-handed grip on his arm that felt good to him. Few people in his life had ever done for him, so here he was soaking this up like a dry sponge. There was no porch. The red bricks laying on their edges went right up to the doorstep and ended. Louise let go long enough to dig the keys from the purse hanging from her left shoulder. Inside, she guided him to an old brown couch that was sunk in where its previous owners had always sat. "Have a seat."

Teddy side-stepped around the end of a marred cherry wood coffee table and collapsed onto the couch.

Louise continued a few paces more to the kitchen. "I'm gonna have some coffee, want some?"

"Sure."

"I'm gonna have some toast and eggs too." She paused to give a cautionary laugh. "You wanna try some?"

Teddy snorted. "You've cleaned up after me enough for one night."

Louise said nothing and continued fixing her breakfast. After a time, she broke the silence. "You gonna be in trouble for not going back to the base?"

Even as murky as his mind was he considered how what he was about to say might sound, but he said it anyway. "I'm on Christmas leave. I don't have to be there for seven days."

"Oh, that's good. I didn't know what else to do with you. I figured if I took you to the base and dumped you out you might get in trouble."

"That's a good possibility. I'll be outta your hair in the morning."

Louise struck Teddy as the kind of girl that might come back with, *you're welcome to my couch for a few days*. But she did not as they both knew where this might go. Instead, she soured the thought. "Kenny wanted me to tell you that you're banned from the Bucket."

Teddy scoffed while acting like losing access to his primary social outlet was no big deal. "Screw him."

Louise adjusted the heat under a cast iron skillet and cracked a couple of eggs in it. Seeing that Teddy was watching, she called out, "Last chance."

"No thanks, I'm good."

"Turn the radio on if you want."

Across the room next to a green padded chair with white stuffing protruding from the right arm was a Philco radio sitting on a low wooden table. To either side of the radio were potted plants. Neither were in flower, just plain leaves.

Teddy sat resting the back of his head on the couch listening to Louise work her scrambled eggs while the coffee percolator wheezed and paused. With no small effort, he finally made his way to the radio and turned it on. Glen Miller's *Moonlight Serenade* was playing.

Louise shouted. "Oh, turn it up. That's my favorite song."

Teddy cranked the volume and returned to the couch. The smell of the coffee, eggs and toast was agreeable to him now. It wasn't so much because he was hungry. It was more than that. It was the feeling he was getting, being here with a girl who would pick him up from a bar room floor and clean the vomit from his face and bring him to her house. Teddy looked over at her. *She's not a beauty queen but then I'm no movie star either.* He knew exactly where his inner self was going with this argument, but he didn't care. *It's like Tony said, pretty girls can't stop looking in the mirror long enough to pay attention to anyone else. They got to have their egos stroked every day.* By and by Teddy convinced himself that Maria was one of those pretty girls that needed her daily dose of adulation and, in his absence, she found someone to provide that. He did not feel guilty for this sudden feeling that he had for Louise. It felt good to cast off some of the sadness and anger Maria had caused him.

And so it began. In the afternoon of the next day while listening to the radio they consummated their lust. Over the next fourteen years they learned to love one another, in spite of Louise not being able to have kids and Teddy's tenth grade education relegating him to hard labor, mostly on ranches. They bounced around ranch to ranch, him a hired hand and her cooking or waitressing in town, if one was nearby. There were many days when Teddy struggled to avoid thinking how he was reliving his past with Agnes.

Louise never complained, right up to that snowy day in December of 1956. She was on her way home to the ranch in southern Idaho where Teddy was working. Ice, on a curve she'd gone around hundreds of times before caught their old pickup. It only rolled once but that was enough to kill her. Memories, too many of them in Idaho, caused Teddy to give Tony a call. *Sure, come on up. I'll put ya to work.*

CHAPTER THIRTY-NINE

August 7, 1965
Sawtooth Club
Pinetop, Montana

Once again, Teddy was drunk. It was a reoccurring Saturday night condition since Louise had died. He was not staggering drunk, but a little wobbly he wouldn't argue with. On occasion, this ritual would be disrupted when Tony invited him up to the big house, as the men called it, for supper. Those evenings usually ran too long to go to town. They'd play checkers, have a few beers and reminisce about the Corps and the war. Tonight, however, Teddy had eaten at the cook shack with the others. It wasn't that this disagreed with him, but the underlying coincidence of Tony's son, Jeff, coming home from college for the summer and Teddy having been invited only once to Saturday supper since then, did.

The bartender leaned back from the conversation with the guys down from Teddy and called out over the jukebox, "You need another Oly?"

Teddy shook his head. "Naw, believe I'll water my lizard and head for the barn."

"Well, watch yourself. I saw the law drive through earlier tonight. You know they pinched old Herb Meyers a week ago. Fined him a hundred bucks is what I heard."

"The hell you say."

"Yeah, they're being pretty hardnosed."

Teddy nodded as he slid off his barstool. "Good to know."

The rest room, the only one that the Sawtooth Club had, was down a short hallway at the back of the room beyond the pool table. Teddy lifted the lid on the toilet and was in the process of relieving himself when *Moonlight Serenade* came on the jukebox. The song always took him back to when he'd met Louise. It was her favorite. About the time he stepped out of the rest room the front door opened and two young guys with long hair, tee shirts, cutoffs and sandals came in laughing like maybe they'd already been drinking. The skinny one's tee shirt had a peace symbol on the front of it, the other one's shirt had a marijuana leaf with the word *Peace,* beneath it. The door had barely closed behind them when the skinny one looked over at the jukebox. He paused as if to focus on the song before saying to his friend, "What is this shit?"

"It's a waltz, dumbass." Marijuana guy then took hold of his friend and started shuffling him around the pool table while laughing.

It was not lost on Teddy that they were making fun of Louise's favorite song. He knew the smart thing to do would be to just keep on walking right out the front door and go home. He'd never been in a bar room fight, not even when he was in the Marines. It just wasn't in his nature. Nonetheless, he started towards the dancers. He was nearly to them when one of the cowboys at the bar who'd been complaining about hippies not wanting to go to Vietnam hollered, "Don't you girls know, dancin' ain't allowed in here?"

The two longhairs immediately stopped laughing, dancing and unhinged one another. Teddy could see the regret in marijuana guy's face even before he had the words out. "Says who?"

The cowboy who was a head taller and probably twenty pounds heavier, stood up from his bar stool. He sneered. "It just became the new rule about thirty seconds ago."

Skinny guy was openly fearful. "Hey man, let's just go."

The cowboy whose denim shirt sleeves were rolled up to the elbows exposing his thick hairy forearms said to marijuana guy, "I believe your friend is giving you some good advice."

Teddy looked on, incredulous, as marijuana guy's fragile ego took hold of his lips. "We came in for a six pack. Once we get it, we'll leave."

The big cowboy laughed causing skinny guy to instantly look ill. A cruel, hateful smile came to the cowboy's face like it was a permanent part of him. "If you ain't out that door in the next ten seconds, I'm gonna whip your ass bad, real bad. Ten – nine –"

Skinny guy blurted, "Screw you, Steve, I'm outta here." He flung the door open and was gone.

"Five – four – three"

Marijuana guy scowled and then bolted through the door.

Teddy couldn't help but laugh. They all did. And for several minutes they retold how it'd been, those hippies being scared shitless. Harry the bartender threw in, *maybe they'll appreciate good music now instead of all this screechy crap they listen* to. They laughed some more, barely noticing the hippies' car when it roared out of Pinetop's one and only street.

Finally, when they'd milked the incident for its entertainment value, Teddy announced before walking out the door, "I'll see you fellas when I see you."

It was mostly dark outside. A single naked lightbulb above the door to the general store across from the Sawtooth was the only evidence of life. The sign at the edge of town said there were 23 people that lived in Pinetop. With the exception of Harry and his patrons, everyone else appeared to be asleep.

Teddy started his pickup, put it in reverse and had gone no more than 15 or 20 feet when he said aloud, "What the hell is going on?"

The question had been rhetorical as his right rear wheel was making a ka-thunking sound. He got out and went around to the other side of his '55 Chevy pickup. The tire was pancaked on one side. His scowl and epithet were simultaneous. "Well, kiss my grits." He gave a deep sigh and was in the process of lifting the spare out of the bed of his pickup when he noticed the Ford truck next to his had an odd tilt to it. He dropped the spare on the ground and went to the Ford. Its right rear tire was flat too. Anger immediately welled up in Teddy. He whispered, "Flat tire my ass." Sobriety was coming to him as he charged back inside.

The big cowboy twisted around on his barstool and laughed, "You come to get one for the road?"

"No, you fellas drivin' the black Ford outside?"

"Yeah."

"Well, you got a flat."

"Ah, for hell sakes. You ain't shitin' me are ya?"

"No Sir, seems these flats are running in pairs."

"Whaddaya mean?"

"I got one too."

From behind the bar, Harry tossed his head to the side so as to give his words emphasis, "Those little pecker necks slashed your tires. I'll bet you a dollar to a pickled dog turd that's what they did."

The big cowboy cut in his voice excited like revenge on the hippies was certain. "Harry didn't you say you saw the law out here earlier tonight?"

"Yeah."

"Well, call the Sheriff. Maybe his man can catch up to these two."

"I could. I saw what they was drivin'."

"Well, call 'em then 'fore those guys get clear outta the country."

Harry reached for a black phone sitting in its cradle not far from the cash register on the backbar. He bent over to read from a piece of paper scotch taped to the counter and began to dial. Soon the phone was ringing. It was audible to the cowboys and Teddy as the jukebox had run dry of quarters and Harry wasn't holding it snug to his ear.

Teddy thought the voice was probably an older woman. "Beaver County Dispatch, how may I help you?"

"Yeah, this is Harry Cooper out at the Sawtooth Club in Pinetop. I wanna report some vandalism."

"What kind of vandalism?"

"Coupla young hippie lookin' guys slashed some tires."

"When did this happen?"

"About ten minutes ago."

"Did you actually see them do this, Sir?"

"Well, no but they got tossed outtta here and right after that one of my customers goes to leave and finds these slashed tires. That doesn't take Sherlock Holmes to figure out who did it."

"Do you know the people that you suspect did this?"

"No. but they was drivin' a dark colored '58 Chevy. They headed north outta here no more than ten minutes ago."

There was a slight pause before the woman replied. "We do have an officer in the area. If I can raise him, I'll pass this on. We've got dead spots out your way, so I can't promise how soon it'll be."

"Harry sighed, "Well, thank you, Ma'am." He hung up the phone.

The big cowboy snorted. "You know, the hell of it is those guys are gonna lie like a used car salesman and that deputy, if he even catches 'em, is gonna have to let 'em go."

"Chalk it up to bad luck," said Teddy as he started for the door. "I'm gonna change my tire and skedaddle for home."

"Want some help?"

"No, appreciate it but I believe I got it."

The big cowboy laughed. "Well, that's good cuz I was hopin' to finish this beer before I go anywhere." He then fished a quarter out of the change on the bar in front of him and gave it to his younger friend. "Go play us some decent music."

It was sometime later when Teddy was struggling in the dark to align the holes in the rim of his spare with the bolts of the bare hub that he heard *Moonlight Serenade,* once again, coming from inside the bar. It caused him to lower the tire to the ground and listen in reverence to Louise. He went back to when they'd had a flat at night and she held the flashlight while he changed it. Tears came to his eyes.

CHAPTER FORTY

On a ranch, Sunday is often no different than any of the other days of the week. In the winter cattle need to be fed and ice chopped so they can drink. Come summer, as it was now, irrigation water needs to be changed and hay baled and stacked before it rains. Today, at 0530, it was irrigation water that needed to be changed. Teddy had just set his canvas dam in the ditch and was in the process of shoveling temporary gaps in the ditch bank to allow the water to run out over the hay stubble when he heard the siren. It was a long way off and not getting much closer. In fact, he couldn't even see the source of it. In his mind's eye, however, he could see some early morning riser coming upon an overnight wreck. He did not envy them.

Tony's shop was located in the end of a big metal Quonset hut. The building was a larger version of what Teddy and Tony had lived in during boot camp. About a third of its interior was occupied by the shop area with the rest used for parking machinery out of the elements during Montana's long cold winters.

It was 0815 when Teddy came around the corner in his personal truck and spotted Jeff standing just inside the shop. He would have kept on going if it wouldn't have been so obvious that he was avoiding him. Teddy stopped just short of the big open doors. Inside was Jeff's blue '59 Chevy Impala. Its trunk lid was up. Through his windshield, Teddy

"

saw Jeff glance over with a look of indifference and then go back to working on his tire. His inner self replied to the look. *Arrogant little shit.* And then he got out and pasted a phony smile on his face out of respect for his time with Tony in the Corps. He called out, "You're up with the chickens."

Jeff looked up as he brushed his long red hair out of his eyes. "Yeah, popped a tire last night on the way home."

Had Jeff not been a mirror image of the hippies at the Sawtooth, Teddy would have told the story of how he came to have a flat tire, instead he said, "Must be catching, I had a blow out last night too."

Jeff came back, "Yeah, guess so." And then he continued applying a hot patch to his tire's inner tube.

Teddy eyed the size of the hole in the tube. "Gonna be tough to get that patch to hold? You might be money ahead to just get a new tube."

"That'd mean a trip to town."

Teddy thought to say something smart-alecky. *Shit, that car of yours has been to town so many times this summer it's worn grooves in the highway.* He said aloud, "I reckon it would."

Jeff lit the patch on fire. It sizzled and flamed and put off an acrid smoke. "I guess this is the vulcanizing part."

Teddy nodded. "I believe it is."

"Well, if it holds till I get back to school that's all I care about."

Not having finished the tenth grade Teddy was intimidated talking about school, but his curiosity got the better of him. "Your father tells me you're studying to be a philosopher."

Jeff frowned. "For now, I am."

Teddy looked mostly serious. "Well, what the hell does a philosopher do? I mean do people pay to have somebody philosophize 'em?"

"You been talkin' to the old man, haven't you?"

"We talk everyday but mostly not about you."

"Well, he wants me to study agriculture and stay on the ranch, but I don't think that's for me."

"So, what is for you?"

"Right now, it's anything that gives me a student deferment."

Teddy flashed back to the conversation at the Sawtooth last night. "I take it you're opposed to the war?"

"So's my dad."

"I know, we've talked."

"Are you?"

It'd been 23 years since Guadalcanal. Seldom a day passed that some image of that time, that place, didn't invade Teddy's mind. He came back. "I don't know. People with more smarts than me think it's a good idea."

"That's the problem, Teddy. These so-called smart people aren't smart at all."

In that instant, Teddy saw himself following the Lieutenant and Sergeant Harper down that road through the jungle towards the woodpecker. It caused him to nod. "Yeah, some of 'em aren't."

"So, you agree with me?"

Teddy forced a laugh. "I better go tend my water."

CHAPTER FORTY-ONE

Between the rumor mill and the Placerville Gazette it became an established fact that Deputy Hank Childers had died while in hot pursuit of someone in violation of the law. However, a full week after his funeral it was still a mystery as to who this might have been.

From his seat high up on the Gleaner Baldwin combine, Teddy saw the Sheriff's car, a black '64 Chevy Impala, drive up to the big house. Because the wheat field he was combining was no more than a quarter mile away, he saw the Sheriff get out of his car and talk to Emma Lou in the front yard where she'd been weeding her flowers. The field Teddy was combining was about a hundred acres. He made almost two full rounds before the Sheriff left in the direction of a pasture where Tony was fixing fence that the bulls had torn down.

About 45 minutes after the Sheriff went over the hill to where Tony was working, he reappeared. As luck would have it, he came through the ranch headquarters at the same time as Teddy was coming in with a truck load of wheat to auger into one of three galvanized steel granaries south of the shop. Teddy was backing up to the metal tub that he dumped the wheat into for the auger to take up when a small cloud of dust rolled over the truck from his blind side. And then the black car, its tall whip antenna still swaying, came into view and stopped. A skinny fifty something man wearing a white straw cowboy hat and a tan short sleeve shirt with a

Beaver County patch on the right shoulder got out. A silver-colored star that said he was the sheriff rested just above his left breast pocket and a pack of Camels. He stood where he was and lit a cigarette while he watched Teddy raise the bed of the truck just enough to ensure a steady flow of grain out the rear end gate.

Teddy cut the truck's engine causing the sheriff to start his way. They met near the front of the truck. The Sheriff stuck his hand out. "Mornin', Charlie Johnson."

Friendly cuss, thought Teddy as he shook hands. "Teddy Walker. You here about the hippies slashin' my tire?"

A blank look came over the Sheriff's face that hinted at being insulted. "No, nuthin's come of that so far. It's about what happened to my deputy."

Teddy felt stupid for bringing up his tire. "Yeah, that was a real sad deal."

Johnson drew thoughtfully on his Camel and then exhaled. "It doesn't make sense, him driving off into that riverbed. I think he was chasing somebody and there was so much dust and he was going so fast, he just couldn't stop."

Teddy came back, respectful of who he was talking to. "If that was the case, you'd think the other fella's car would've been piled up too."

"That would be a normal person's conclusion but I'm thinkin' the person driving this other car was touched in the head. I think they were so desperate to get away they risked death to do it."

"So, you think this other car just sailed over that dry crik?"

"I know it did. We found broken pieces of a bracket for a shock absorber. And there were tracks like maybe somebody changed a tire."

A pulse of concern, unfounded or not, came over Teddy. "Well, Sheriff, I drive an old Chevy pickup that a man on a good horse could probably catch so I'm not sure why you're talkin' to me."

Johnson smiled briefly before ratcheting up the intensity of his demeanor. "This is just between us girls, alright?"

Teddy nodded. "Sure."

"I've got two suspects in this case. One of them is the hippies you had a run-in with around midnight at the Sawtooth in Pinetop. Harry says they left there like a bat out of hell. So, maybe they go on like that and Deputy Childers picks 'em up on radar and goes after 'em. Or, my other suspect is your boss's son. The only thing that draws me to him is he's got a history of speeding and he has cause to drive the road where the chase likely started. So, my question to you is, was Jeff Halvorson home when you got here the night all of this happened?"

The answer, the truthful one anyway, came to Teddy right away. On the night in question, he had been lying in bed listening to the radio. He'd not been there long, but too much had happened that night for sleep to come easy. Even if he had been asleep, Jeff's car was loud. It would've woke him up as it had on a number of other nights. He remembered exactly what time it was that Jeff came home as the glass pack mufflers on his car gave him away. He'd checked his watch. *0135, Damned kid.* And now, Jeff's blown tire took on a new meaning. Seeing the Sheriff's suspicious stare, Teddy blurted out, "I'm trying to think, Sheriff. I've slept since then." He paused. This would devastate Tony, his friend in boot camp when the others turned on him. His friend at Pendleton and on Guadalcanal and now the guy who'd propped him up after Louise had been killed. Finally, his conscience wouldn't allow him to say anything else. "You know Sheriff, I just can't say for certain. I tooled on by the big house that night and went down to my little trailer by the crik and went to bed."

If they'd been playing poker, Johnson would've went all in. "You pretty certain of that?"

"Yes Sir, it's kinda comin' back to me."

"Do you remember what time you got home?"

"Teddy scrunched up his face like he was trying to remember. "A little after one, I think."

Johnson's expression became wry. "One, huh?"

"As best I recall it was."

"You know it's too damned bad that Jeff and his friend decided to pack into the Bob Marshal Wilderness just now."

The Sheriff's words struck Teddy as loaded, even taunting, but it was like his mother had once told him, *one lie begets another lie*. He came back with what Tony had told him. "Yeah, I guess he's gonna do some fishing 'fore he goes back to school."

Johnson puffed on his cigarette and then took it away resting the palm of that hand on the butt of his Smith & Wesson revolver that was snug against his right hip. He looked off at the timber covered mountains beyond Teddy. His tone was wistful but disingenuous. "Yes Sir, it'd sure be nice to be able to go fishing for a week at the drop of a hat."

Teddy felt like he was being toyed with. *He knows I lied. He knows it*. He continued the game. "I may do the same when we get the crops in."

Johnson took a final draw on his cigarette and then blew the smoke out in an exasperated manner. He tossed the butt in the powdery dirt before grinding it under his boot heel. "Well, I guess when the boy comes back, we'll have us a chat cause God only knows when I could find him in the Bob." He paused and laughed. "But hey, I could take my fishing pole and go look for him on the county's nickel."

Teddy did his best to hide the fact that he was fearful and a liar. "Sounds like you want to talk to Jeff pretty bad."

The Sheriff nodded. "I do, I do for a fact want to talk to that boy." And then he walked away.

Teddy watched Johnson drive off. He felt sick, kind of like that day on Guadalcanal when they were walking up the road towards the woodpecker.

It had taken about a half hour to unload the truck. Teddy was now on the far end of the wheat field squinting his eyes and sometimes holding his breath against the dry chaff that was boiling up in front of him. The chaff, it seemed, wasn't as bad since his conversation with the Sheriff had caused him to be detached with worry. Suddenly, he realized there was standing grain to either side of the big paddle reel. He cursed aloud, "Oh, shit" as he brought the combine back from its meander. It wasn't much, a sliver maybe a foot wide but close to a hundred yards long. And then right on time to ensure his screwup would not go unnoticed was Tony's pickup parked next to the grain truck. Teddy's mind, however, was in a different place. *He's scared a what I said.* On the way there, he rehearsed how it would go. None of the outcomes were good.

Teddy shut the combine down straight across from the grain truck and began to empty his hopper into the truck like it was just another day of harvesting wheat. Tony, on the other hand, walked with some urgency around the combine and climbed the metal ladder to Teddy's perch. He went right to it. "Emma Lou tells me you and the Sheriff had a talk."

Teddy could see the fear in Tony's eyes. It was obvious, intense. He felt sorry for him, having a son that would cause this kind of angst. He came back in a hard voice. "I didn't tell him anything that will hurt Jeff."

Tony frowned. "Meaning what?"

"Told him I just didn't notice if Jeff was home or not when I came in."

Tony snorted. "You told him you didn't notice a bright blue car with polished chrome rims sitting right in front of the house beneath our yard light? That's what you told him?"

Teddy could see Tony's fear had evolved to anger. He responded in kind. "I cudda told him the truth, that Jeff didn't get home till well past one. Would that suit ya?"

Tony came back quick and sharp, ignoring what had once existed between them. "A smart guy, a friend, would have read between the lines and told Johnson that Jeff was home when you got here. I mean you gotta figure if Jeff was here, he couldn't have done whatever it is that Johnson thinks he did."

"You mean run from that deputy that got killed where the bridge was out?"

The sudden gravity of the situation caused Tony to go silent.

Teddy, however, did not stop in the destruction of their friendship. "You know my ass is hanging out here. Those damned glass packed mufflers of Jeff's came up at breakfast that morning. They woke Cecil and Harvey up. And I said, me too. And they groused about it being almost 1:30. We'll all be in a world of shit if the Sheriff talks to those two."

Fear came back to Tony's face. He shook his head. "Damned kid."

Teddy softened his tone. "Well, the Sheriff is just waiting for Jeff to come back from the Bob."

"He ain't coming back."

"What?"

"He's going to Canada."

"That might make things worse."

"Told him that, but he's gotten himself mixed up with some bad people over in Billings."

"Drugs?"

"All he would say is that it would be best if he left the country."

The old Teddy said, "I'm sorry."

For a time, Tony said nothing before looking over at the uncut sliver of wheat. A weak grin came to his face as Teddy's eyes followed. "You takin' a nap?"

Teddy grinned back. "Just a short one."

They both laughed, but they knew things were different now.

EPILOGUE

November 7, 1965

Sheriff Johnson was no fool. Even before Jeff's friend came out of the wilderness, he had alerted the Canadian authorities to be on the lookout for Jeff. However, the plan to be safely into Canada before the law in Montana was any the wiser blew up on the Blackfeet Indian Reservation just north of Browning. Jeff had walked out of the mountains and hitch-hiked almost to the border. Unfortunately for him, his next ride turned out to be a tribal policeman who had his picture. The cop became a celebrity when it was discovered Jeff had 40 pounds of pot in his pack. That discovery explained why a person would risk death jumping his car over a dry creek bed. However, in exchange for Jeff telling his pot source, the state agreed to drop the charge against him for failure to stop for a law officer. The judge gave him five years in the state prison at Deerlodge. It was a decision that didn't sit well with a lot of people, especially Hank Childers' family. The blow-back to Tony, Marine war hero or not, was considerable.

After the crops were in and they'd rounded the cattle up off the forest and shipped the calves, Teddy moved on. It wasn't on bad terms, but it was necessary, nonetheless. He'd had to be a liar, a dishonest person at Tony's place, and that was something he couldn't justify to himself, not even for friendship.

It was around four in the afternoon when he got into Elko. Billy had told him on the phone that he would meet him at the Ruby Mountains Casino. *I'll be at the bar.*

Teddy pushed against the big glass cylinder door and rotated around until it spit him out into a sea of bright lights, cigarette smoke and a din of shouts and laughter, buzzers and coins hitting metal. To his left he spied the bar. A man wearing a light green down coat with a sizeable duct tape patch on the back was sitting there. The crown of his gray Stetson was ringed with sweat, stains and dirt. *That's gotta be him.* Teddy started across the plush red carpet towards the man. He was nearly to him when they spotted one another in the mirror behind the bar. They broke into smiles. Billy had grown a walrus moustache since his days as a Marine, that was black as coal. He twisted around on his bar stool and slid off favoring his right leg. "Hey, you made 'er."

Teddy pumped his friend's hand. "It's a long ride in that old jalopy of mine."

Billy laughed. "And we still gotta go about half-way to Jarbridge tonight."

"Hell, if you'd gave me directions I wudda drove out there on my own. Saved you a trip to town."

A big grin came to Billy's face. "Well, I just didn't want to be accused of leading a tenderfoot astray out in the wilds of Nevada."

They both laughed. Billy came back. "Follow me."

Billy took his beer from the bar and started off across the casino with a noticeable limp. Teddy fell in beside him. "Where we headed?"

"I wanna introduce you to somebody from our days in the Corps."

"Who?"

"You'll see."

On they went past the craps table with its lone player. *Shooter coming out. Eight, easy eight..* At the beginning of the blackjack tables, that were better attended, they turned right into a maze of slot machines. To their left an old white-haired woman with a cigarette dangling from her lips methodically fished nickels from a carboard cup, stuffed them two at a time into her machine and pulled the handle with no result. Teddy thought she looked pitiful. *Either here spending her social security or home watching soaps.* And then they emerged from the slots at the entrance to the coffee shop. The red carpet gave way to beige tile. The hostess, a young woman, greeted them. "Table for two."

"No, just one," said Billy.

Surprised, Teddy blurted, "What?"

"You'll see. I'll be at the bar."

Teddy fell in behind the hostess. They'd not quite reached his table when he spotted her and she him. Twenty-three years had passed and she was still as pretty as the first time he'd seen her at the Rusty Bucket.

Her smile was big and genuine but reserved. "Hello, Teddy. Billy said you were coming."

His eyes had not purposely gone there, but it was hard to overlook the diamond on her left hand. "It's good to see you. I always wondered what happened to you."

"I wondered about you too until I ran into Billy a few weeks ago. I'm sorry about Louise."

Teddy nodded. "She was a good person. My friend for life."

"Those are the best kind to have."

"I wrote to you, lots of times."

"I know, but I was too ashamed to write back."

Teddy did not feel the pain that he once imagined he would when this day came. Louise insulated him from that. "I guess it all worked out for the best."

"Yes, I'm married with three kids."

"Sounds like you're happy."

"Yes, very."

It wasn't that he wanted her back, but Teddy was beginning to feel sad. He guessed it was due mostly to not having Louise. With her he could deal with anything that came his way. They were a team. Now, it was different. He said, before she asked him if he was happy, "I guess I better go. Me and Billy have got a ways to go tonight."

"Wait, don't leave. I have something for you. You'll wait, won't you?"

Teddy nodded. "Ok, I'll be right here."

Maria went behind the counter and took an envelope from her purse. She returned in spite of the hostess seating a couple in her section. She opened the envelope and handed Teddy a black and white photo. "Tell me what you think."

Teddy studied the photo, first not wanting and then wanting to believe it. "How old is he?"

"Twenty-three."

"What's his name?"

"Teddy."

He looked at her, unable to say it. *All these years I had a son.*

She came back. "I'm sorry." She added, "You can write to him. He's in the Army in Vietnam. His address is in that envelope."

Teddy looked at the address. "Sergeant, huh?"

"Yes, he's done well."

Silence filled with recollections and what-ifs filled the space between them.

From across the room the hostess shouted. "Maria."

Teddy glanced over, there was Kenny behind the bar at the Rusty Bucket.

Maria jolted him back. "You'll write him?"

"Yeah, I'll write him. I'll write him tonight."

And for the first time since Louise died, Teddy didn't hurt quite as much.

ABOUT THE AUTHOR

John Hansen is a retired wildlife biologist and wildland firefighter. Since retiring in 2014 he has written a dozen books that have won numerous awards. He and his wife Debi and their rescue dog Bella and three-legged cat, Gizmo live in western Montana. For more information on John's work go to: http://johnhansen.net/